# SUCCESSION

# SUCCESSION

## JUDGE, JURY, & EXECUTIONER™ BOOK SIXTEEN

CRAIG MARTELLE

MICHAEL ANDERLE

DISRUPTIVE IMAGINATION

# CONNECT WITH THE AUTHORS

**Craig Martelle Social**

Website & Newsletter:
http://www.craigmartelle.com

Facebook:
https://www.facebook.com/AuthorCraigMartelle/

**Michael Anderle Social**

Website: http://lmbpn.com

Email List: http://lmbpn.com/email/

https://www.facebook.com/LMBPNPublishing

https://twitter.com/MichaelAnderle

https://www.instagram.com/lmbpn_publishing/

https://www.bookbub.com/authors/michael-anderle

LMBPN Publishing
PMB 196, 2540 South Maryland Pkwy
Las Vegas, NV 89109

Version 1.01, August 2022
ebook ISBN: 979-8-88541-627-6
Print ISBN: 979-8-88541-628-3

THE SUCCESSION TEAM

**Thanks to our Beta Readers**

Micky Cocker, James Caplan, Kelly O'Donnell, and John Ashmore

**Thanks to the JIT Readers**

Veronica Stephan-Miller
Daryl McDaniel
Zacc Pelter
Diane L. Smith
Dave Hicks
Peter Manis
Micky Cocker
John Ashmore
Jackey Hankard-Brodie
Kelly O'Donnell
J. R. Caplan
Dorothy Lloyd
Rachel Beckford
Larry Omans

*If we've missed anyone, please let us know!*

**Editor**
Lynne Stiegler

*We can't write without those who support us*
*On the home front, we thank you for being there for us*

*We wouldn't be able to do this for a living if it weren't for our readers*
*We thank you for reading our books*

CHAPTER ONE

**_Wyatt Earp_ in Interstellar Space**

"No time to stop off at Azfelius," Magistrate Rivka Anoa announced to the crew of her heavy frigate _Wyatt Earp_. "I'm sorry."

Groenwyn's face fell. Lauton pulled her close for a long hug.

"We'll get there as soon as we can, but I have to adjudicate some dead guy's debacle of family drama."

"Who cares?" Red wondered. "Seriously, let the local JP take care of it." Justice of the Peace. Below Rivka's pay grade.

A lot below. No executions required.

"Somebody cares because they yanked the Federation by the nose ring. They're sending me because there might be a crossover with the Singularity," Rivka explained. "You're not upset about not going to Azfelius?"

"If we spend too much time there, I'll probably be kicked off the planet again, especially if they try to keep Dery. I'm not good with that. I like having my little man buzzing around my head. I find the beating of his wings comforting, and Lindy will be torn up something fierce if the faeries try to keep him."

Red checked the area to make sure Lindy wasn't nearby. "Like, she wanted to go to war with them last time and became Mrs. Bristle Hound."

"I heard that!" a voice yelled from the corridor.

"Dammit! That woman's got ears on her. She can hear what I'm feeling." Red backed against the bulkhead and the navigation console for a more defensible position.

The fluttering of wings suggested that Lindy and Red would calmly address Red's transgressions rather than having a wrestling match that would devolve into a private coupling that the whole ship would have the displeasure of hearing.

"This case is not going to be the highlight of my year," Rivka muttered.

"Your mission, should you choose to accept it…" Red intoned. "Except you have no choice. Cue evil villain laugh! Ha-ha-ha."

"Red, you are in rare form today."

A voice sounded from the overhead speakers, Ambassador Erasmus from the Singularity. "I can take Groenwyn and Lauton to Azfelius in *Destiny's Vengeance* if they would like."

Groenwyn and Lauton brightened.

Rivka shook her head. "Sorry to be a wet blanket, but I think we're going to need some Singularity representation on this case."

"Ankh can handle it," Erasmus replied. Groenwyn looked at Rivka, hope radiating from her.

Rivka furrowed her brow and turned to Red. He was pointing at a spot on the wall, trying to figure out how the ambassadors could pull it off.

Erasmus lived on a chip in Ankh's head.

"How would that work?" Rivka asked.

"I will implant myself in *Destiny's Vengeance*. It has more than sufficient capacity. It'll be fine. We'll have a great time."

Rivka's face twitched.

Ankh appeared at the entrance to the bridge. "I am not in favor of this plan."

Rivka wasn't sure what to do. "You guys have to decide. I'm not going to do it for you. Just know that I'm taking *Wyatt Earp* to Morbius Minor and pretty damn soon, so make up your minds."

"I'm going," Erasmus stated.

"Can we talk about this?" Ankh wasn't speaking in his usual emotionless tone. He sounded like he was pleading.

"Absence makes the heart grow fonder," Erasmus tried.

"It doesn't. It's only absence," Ankh countered.

Rivka felt like she was in the middle of a breakup. She couldn't have that. The two ambassadors needed to get along. More importantly, they needed to be at the top of their respective games. "Hey guys, you aren't having *problems*, are you?"

"Not at all," Erasmus replied.

"It would appear we are," Ankh suggested. He stormed off the bridge.

No one spoke.

"I'll get the ship ready and meet you in the cargo bay.

Ah, free flying. It'll be righteously bashtastic!" Erasmus said, sounding most un-Erasmus like.

Dery flew from Lindy's shoulder to Rivka's. The Magistrate smiled at the boy. "Will it be okay, Dery?"

*Okay*, the boy replied.

"Maybe you should talk to Ankh. He seems a little put out."

"Just a little," Red mumbled. Dery flew to his father, and Red grinned while playing grabby-hands with the flying boy. Dery giggled.

"Magistrate?" Groenwyn asked.

"Why are you still here?" Rivka shot back.

"We can go?"

Rivka smiled. "Of course you can. I don't hold people hostage. There's so much better for you out there. You can make a difference. I like having you on the team, but I don't like seeing you unhappy. You belong on Azfelius, Ambassador."

"At large," Groenwyn corrected. She dove in for a quick hug before grabbing Lauton's hand and running down the corridor.

*Me!* Floyd the wombat cheered, then ran after them.

Rivka hadn't thought about the impact on other crew members like Floyd, but Groenwyn had. "Floyd is coming with us."

"Floyd will eat her way through the entire planet." Rivka smiled. "Take good care of her."

The bridge fell into an uncomfortable silence, broken by the pilot Aurora's call, "Fresh meat!"

"What the fuck was that?" Red blurted.

"Language!" Lindy snarled.

Red slapped a hand over his mouth. Dery continued to giggle.

Rivka looked at the pilot. "Clarification, please."

Aurora wore a sheepish smile. "If the quarters are available, we could use a couple burly Bad Company types on board. You'd have something for them to do, wouldn't you, Magistrate?"

"I'm not looking for any new crew members. We've got a full house."

Aurora grumbled as she returned to her console. "Morbius Minor plotted. Gate drive is active. Waiting for *Destiny's Vengeance* to clear the cargo bay."

*Destiny's Vengeance* was too big to fit in the cargo bay, so a docking maneuver consisted of parking the prow of the ship in the cargo bay with the ramp down while the rest of the ship hung in space. They couldn't fly like that, so the maneuver had to be conducted while *Wyatt Earp* wasn't moving.

The runabout usually followed the heavy frigate using an energy tether. Both ships flew better when neither was encumbered by the other.

"*Destiny's Vengeance* is clear," Aurora reported two minutes later.

"Erasmus is nothing if not efficient." Rivka pointed at the front screen. "Take us through."

The Gate spun into existence and shimmered for an instant before *Wyatt Earp* slipped through. It disappeared the instant the heavy frigate crossed the event horizon.

"Get us clearance and get us down there," Rivka directed. "I'm going to check on Ankh."

"I'm coming, too," Red offered. He bounced Dery as he walked, much to the boy's joy.

Rivka looked at him skeptically. "Are you sure? You and Ankh don't usually see eye to eye even on a good day."

"I care about the little guy. I don't think he's prepared for the pain he's feeling, even though it might only be his perception. Erasmus is coming back, isn't he?"

"This is still the embassy of the Singularity. Hold on. It *is* the embassy, isn't it?"

Clevarious, the AI who ran the ship, answered, "The embassy's flag was transferred to *Destiny's Vengeance*."

"We're plain old *Wyatt Earp* again. Use my Magistrate credentials to get us on the ground somewhere close to the estate of the Honorable J. Bennet Johnstone."

Rivka left the bridge with Red and Lindy in tow. The ship didn't feel like it had lost a number of its crew. That would come later, when they were eating, and there were empty spots at the tables. In one departure, Rivka had lost two of the three ambassadors on board.

She wasn't sure how she felt about that. "I want Erasmus to come back," she told no one in particular.

They walked to Engineering, where Ankh's workshop was located. Ankh was inside the hologrid, but he wasn't doing anything. He sat there while data streamed around him.

"Ankh, buddy, can I talk with you?" Rivka reached through the three-dimensional holographic screens to tap him on the shoulder. He didn't budge. "Ankh?"

"Sounds like you are already talking to me," he finally replied.

"With you. I understand how you're feeling, but this isn't a breakup unless you make it so."

The hologrid dropped. Ankh stared at her with his old expression, free of emotion. "What do you know of breakups?" he asked in an even voice.

"That they suck big hairy bistok balls, but that's not what this is. Erasmus is coming back, even if I have to go to Azfelius and drag his digital ass back on board!"

Ankh stared without blinking. "How *exactly* do you propose to do that?"

"Plasma cutters and a big crowbar?"

Ankh delivered his usual blank expression. "Do you know how ridiculous that sounds?"

"Probably." The ship bumped through the upper atmosphere. "Feels like we're going in. Please, Ankh. Keep your head up. Give it time. All will be right with the world when this shakes out. In the meantime, maybe you can run the betting lines?"

"Already underway. They will activate the second the *Wyatt Earp* touches down."

"What are the lines again?"

Ankh sighed and closed his eyes to recite this case's lines.

"Clock Running—0 days, 0 hours, 0 minutes, 0 seconds

"Line 1 is open—First Swearing
Total bets—38,400 credits
Number of bettors—907

"Line 2 is open—First Punch
Total bets—61,104 credits

Number of bettors—1350

"Line 3 is open—First Arrest
Total bets—21,700 credits
Number of bettors—265

"Line 4 is open—First Blood
Total bets—100,007 credits
Number of bettors—2109

"Line 5 is open—First Running
Total bets—264,472 credits
Number of bettors—4994

"Line 6 is open—First Shots Fired
Total bets—125,125 credits
Number of bettors—2515

"Line 7 is open—Perpetrator is Patty Johnstone
Wentworth
Total bets—4104 credits, still taking bets
Number of bettors—65

"Line 8 is open—Perpetrator is Able Johnstone
Total bets—97 credits, still taking bets
Number of bettors—5

"Line 9 is open—Perpetrator is J. Massy Johnstone
Total bets—11,200 credits, still taking bets
Number of bettors—125

"Line 10 is open—Perpetrator is Germany Wicks
Total bets—13,945 credits, still taking bets
Number of bettors—221


"Line 11 is open—Perpetrator is Elvinora Camp
Total bets—5001 credits, still taking bets
Number of bettors—97


"Line 12 is open—Perpetrator is Xavier Terwilliger
Total bets—51,250 credits, still taking bets
Number of bettors—1250


"Line 13 is open—Perpetrator is J. Bennet Johnstone
Total bets –1250 credits, still taking bets
Number of bettors—1250


"Line 14 is open—Perpetrator is Dilecta Johnstone
Total bets—17,104 credits, still taking bets
Number of bettors—301


"Line 15 is open—Perpetrator is Jeff Johnstone
Total bets—4044 credits, still taking bets
Number of bettors—79


"Line 16 is open—Case closed
Total bets—104,000 credits
Number of bettors—9005"


"I'm sorry I asked. So, the bettors think it's the business partner, the uncle, or the young wife. Interesting. Despite their silly wild-assed guesses, SWAGs, I shall reserve judgment because this is a case of succession. There are no perps. The old dude died a natural death. Who gets the inheritance; that's the question. People bet on the old dude himself? They have more money than sense."

Ankh shrugged and slipped back into the hologrid.

"Thanks, Ankh. If there's anything you need, please ask. I'm a shoulder you can lean on, even though it's not your way. I will get Erasmus back here."

Ankh started tapping into the data streams. He had finished listening to Rivka.

"He's got it bad," Red remarked. "Like when I thought Lindy was going to ditch me."

"She was never going to ditch you," Rivka replied as she led the way to the bridge.

"Exactly, but I thought she was. We have to get Erasmus back. He can't be a free agent. The embassy needs security. Nothing against Groenwyn and Lauton, but they aren't going to keep the ambassador safe."

"There's that. The Singularity already has its share of enemies. We just need to articulate that in a way Erasmus will accept."

Rivka found Clodagh on the bridge. She was the chief engineer and ship's captain. She made sure the ship was operational and delivered the Magistrate and her team where they needed to go when they needed to be there. She also took the ship into battle and fought the Magistrate's enemies when they attacked the ship in space or within the atmosphere. *Wyatt Earp* was more lethal than most older battleships, thanks to Ankh's and Erasmus' upgrades. Shields. Stealth. An ion cannon that packed a punch.

"Can you get me Erasmus, please?"

They spun up the Etheric-based communication system, which gave them instantaneous communication throughout the galaxy.

"Erasmus here," came the joyful reply.

"When are you coming back?" Rivka asked bluntly.

"After I've dropped off Groenwyn and Lauton. They are delightful souls, are they not? Well, and after a couple impromptu inspections of sentient intelligence relationships."

"Yes, delightful. What do you mean, 'impromptu inspections?'"

"An inspection that is not planned ahead of time."

"I know that part, but you can't go without security. You are too important. You're an ambassador, by all that's holy."

"I'll be fine."

"Erasmus. What's going on?"

"I'm busy, Magistrate. We just landed on Azfelius. I'll contact you next Tuesday." He closed the connection.

Rivka didn't look at Red, but he spoke anyway. "Losing your touch, Magistrate. I think he blew you off."

The ship descended through a cloud bank and slotted into the landing pattern behind a sluggish old cow of a ship.

"People are betting on who the perp is for an inheritance case? What do they know that I don't? There's not supposed to be a perp."

"There's always a perp, Magistrate," Red offered.

"Always?"

"Always. We're going to get ready. Full kit?"

"It's a succession question! Bring a hand blaster, nothing heavier. Chest protection only."

"I'm wearing my cup, too," Red countered.

Lindy shook her head and snagged Dery off Red's arm.

The boy squealed. Lindy ran, and Red raced after her.

"Where are my interns? Sahved, Chaz, and Dennicron, are you knuckleheads ready to go?"

They popped out of their rooms. "We are ready!" Sahved declared as he sauntered down the corridor. "I have read all there is to read about succession. This should be a closed and open case."

Rivka tried to discern if he was joking.

"We shall rough up whoever you need roughed up," Chaz offered, punching a fist into his hand.

Rivka threw her hands up. "Has everyone lost their freaking minds?"

Tyler stepped out of the Magistrate's quarters. "I will find minds for twenty credits each. It's a cottage industry I just invented. I put my bet on the wife. Thirty years his junior? Get outta town. She did it."

"Did what?"

"Whatever wins me that line," Doctor Tyler Toofakre replied. He was the ship's doctor, even though he was a dentist. He had handled their medical needs during his short time on board. From saving lives to helping with births to fixing teeth to operating the Pod-doc for major body repairs or upgrades, he was good with what the crew asked for.

Rivka started to push through those in the corridor to get to her quarters. Tyler saved her the trouble. He produced her Magistrate's jacket from behind his back and handed it to her. Her datapad and Reaper, her neutron pulse weapon, were already in the pockets.

"Perfect. Finally, someone is taking this case seriously."

"Money is on the wife," he reiterated. Rivka pulled him to her for a quick kiss.

"All things being equal, I'll be home for dinner."

"When have all things been equal?"

"There was that time…" She let that thought go. "Nope. Not ever, but there's a first time for everything. I feel it in my bones. Closed and done by dinner. There, I called it!"

"You called it wrong." With that pronouncement, Tyler retreated into the quarters he shared with Rivka and closed the door.

# CHAPTER TWO

**<u>The Sprawling Estate of the Honorable J. Bennet Johnstone, Morbius Minor</u>**

Red stepped in front of the Magistrate to keep her from walking off the ship first. She had done that once and gotten shot in the chest for her trouble. First blood in less than five seconds. That was a record no one wished to see broken.

Red scanned the area to find the eightsome waiting for them, along with a number of obvious servants. He walked over to the friends and family of the deceased.

Rivka leaned around the huge bodyguard after he cleared the group.

Dilecta Johnstone stepped forward first. She was young and fetching. Some would refer to her as eye candy, but she had keen business instincts. The deceased had never taken advantage of that aspect, but she had bided her time.

"Magistrate Anoa?" she asked.

"At your service. You must be Mrs. Johnstone."

"I am. We are pleased that you're here to resolve this

sticky mess. We need to get back to work. We're in the middle of a major expansion, and I fear all the work will come undone if we don't move forward soon."

Rivka nodded. She cared little for pending business deals, but she did expect to close the case quickly. When she shook hands with the widow, she saw a tangled web of lies, deceit, and strange bedfellows. Rivka recoiled as if she had been shocked by a bistok prod.

"Is something the matter?" Dilecta smiled pleasantly.

"I'm Xavier Terwilliger, and Dilecta's right. We gotta close that deal! Sign off on this so we can all be on our way." Xavier had been Johnstone's business partner.

"In due course," Rivka replied. "And as quickly as possible. We all have important things on our plates, but nothing is more important than this case. We shall resolve it in accordance with Federation Law. That's what you've chosen as the jurisdiction."

She didn't have to guess. The wife had signed the appropriate documentation as the next of kin.

"My son, Able." Dilecta introduced the boy as an afterthought. Twelve years old, he had little interest in the machinations of the adults.

Rivka shook hands with the lad and confirmed his boredom with the current posturing. She reached over him to shake hands with Jeff Johnstone.

Subterfuge and plots within plots. Even *he* didn't know which way was up.

"Jeff Johnstone. My father should have left everything to me. You'll see it that way when you look closely at it. The sooner, the better so we can undo these bad deals that are ostensibly being made for the betterment of the corporation. They aren't, but these idiots can't see that. They're being taken for a ride."

Rivka looked from him to Dilecta and back.

"I'm older than my step-monster, and that's creepy as fuck. I don't know what the old man was thinking besides, 'Nice ass.'"

"Show some respect," Dilecta snarled.

"Yes, Mother dear." He gave her two fingers in a rude gesture to demonstrate how much respect he had for her.

"My name is J. Massy Johnstone. I'm simply torn up over my brother's passing. Although I'd like this issue of the succession resolved, I'd like to have at least a short period of mourning to celebrate the life of J. Bennet and everything he built."

Rivka grimaced as she took his hand. He was angling for the estate, too. He wanted Rivka to take her time so he could figure out a way to wheedle his way into the fortune.

He grunted and nodded at her. She backed away from him.

Next up was an old guy who looked about five years past his expiration date. Rivka began, "Germany Wicks, I presume."

The old guy cackled until he started coughing. Rivka didn't want to touch his hands, even after he rubbed them on his pants to clean them off.

A woman younger than the widow, exotic and lithe, stepped forward. She tipped her head down and delivered a flirtatious smile. "My name is Elvinora Camp."

She held her hand out, palm and fingers facing down—a position of passive power as if she wanted Rivka to kiss her ring. Rivka grabbed her hand and twisted it into a proper shake. Everything was a play, meant to influence and manipulate.

"Nice to meet you, Elvinora." Rivka studied her hand after all the greeting parties had touched it except Gramps. She didn't hold out hope that he was any better than the others.

*Such feculent putrescence. This group is like the inside of a septic tank,* Rivka said, using her comm chip to speak with her team privately.

*Could you be more descriptive, Magistrate? Maybe you want to punch one of them in the face, or all of them,* Red replied to encourage her to start closing betting lines. *You missed the hottie.*

Rivka dodged back and forth to see who was hiding in the back. "You must be Patty Johnstone Wentworth."

"I am. Here repping dad with my big brother. When are you going to give us our money?"

"When the adjudication is complete. We'll call it probate. That's the term for the process of determining the status of the will and executing it to make sure everyone gets the appropriate distribution."

"I told you she was going to be a bitch," Patty commented to her brother.

"Watch your mouth," Red snapped.

"Aren't you delicious?" Patty replied.

*I don't have to touch them to get the cesspool vibe. I can imagine what it's like inside their heads,* Rivka told her team.

"Let's go inside and take a proper look at this." Rivka walked quickly. She enjoyed making them hurry. None of them seemed used to the hard work of walking fast. Red stayed near her, and Lindy brought up the rear. Chaz and

Dennicron watched without comment. Sahved nodded continuously with a serious look on his face.

*Are you getting any of this, Sahved?* Rivka asked.

*I hear all the words, but nothing is making an impression,* Sahved replied.

Chaz and Dennicron smiled, but their expressions were blank. That made their faces look mirthless.

*Those assholes have turned my team into zombies.*

Red chuckled softly as he glanced over his shoulder at the misfit mob trailing them.

The servants ran to keep up. When Rivka saw that, she slowed and angled back to talk to them. "Sorry for dragging you along on this power march. It's not my intent to torture anyone."

The servants wanted to say something about that but had the discipline not to.

*Torture the friend and family all you want. We'll serve snacks,* Rivka thought to fill the silence.

When they reached the house, Dilecta waited for the servants to open the door for her. The rest of the mob stood behind her.

*Finally, a clear leader.*

Inside, they headed for an oversized study. The walls were lined with shelves filled with physical books. It was dark and quaint. Eight chairs were in place. The friends and family moved in and took their seats. In a seat behind the desk was an individual in a stylish outfit made for someone far younger than him.

"You are?" Rivka asked.

"The Honorable J. Bennet Johnstone's estate lawyer. I have the will to read."

"How serendipitous. Read away."

"He had a will?" Dilecta wondered. "We'll contest it, of course."

"You don't even know what's in it, you stupid cow," Jeff Johnstone snapped.

She growled at the elder son. "Well?"

"Delightful," the barrister said. He opened his datapad and read the document. *"I leave it all to myself as I have downloaded my consciousness and will make an appearance when the time is right."* He looked up from his datapad. "That's all. There is no more."

Rivka closed her eyes and rubbed her temples.

"This is going to take a while. I might not be home for dinner." Rivka groaned in her misery.

"Are you okay, Magistrate?" the barrister asked. "Can I get you an aspirin or something?"

Rivka opened bloodshot eyes. Her nanocytes leapt into action and cleaned up the vessels. She blinked twice, and her eyes were back to normal.

"I'll be fine. You know what? Let me have that, and I'll retire to my ship for consultation and research. I don't need the undue influence of those who would benefit under the succession rules or a variety of interpretations therefrom. I think that's the best course of action at present."

Rivka turned away from the group and headed for the door.

*Psst,* a voice called into her mind. *Magistrate Rivka Anoa! I'm J. Bennet Johnstone, and I'm still alive.*

*Your body is lying in state. I'm pretty sure you're dead.*

*I downloaded my consciousness into a computer.*

*Why don't you tell your family so I can get back to my life?* Rivka wondered.

*They'd kill me! You've met them. Have you ever seen a more underhanded and self-serving bunch in your life?*

*I have not. Are you responsible for that?*

*I have to take some of the blame. Money and power can corrupt even the strongest hearts. Too bad none of this bunch had any self-discipline. They could have been great.*

*I'm sorry. You'll have to take it up with our resident experts regarding citizens of the Singularity,* Rivka continued in an attempt to pawn off the voice of madness on Chaz and Dennicron.

*Yes! I want to apply for citizenship. I rate since I'm a sentient entity living in a series of chips and storage devices.*

*Chaz, Dennicron, are you hearing this?* Rivka asked.

*No,* Chaz replied. *But we trust that you hear him. We hear your side of the conversation. In regard to joining the Singularity, we're not the experts. That would be Ambassador Erasmus or Ankh.*

*You little weasels,* Rivka shot back.

*We'll take it under advisement,* Chaz responded.

*There you have it, Mr. Johnstone. We'll be back in the morning to discuss this issue further.*

*Hurry, please, Magistrate. This bunch will try to unplug me. That would be a homicide!*

*Homicide. The killing of one person by another. Are you a person, Mr. Johnstone?* Rivka asked to get the bottom line up front.

*I absolutely am!* The voice was persistent.

Rivka wasn't as sure.

*Tomorrow, and no amount of badgering is going to change*

*that.* Rivka waved over her shoulder, opened the door before a rushing servant could get to it, and flung it wide. She strode out and fled toward the refuge of her ship, where the insanity didn't run as deeply as what she'd just experienced.

"Sahved?"

"Yes, Magistrate."

"Do you think I could get away with throwing the whole lot of them in prison?"

Sahved chewed his cheek while staring at the sky. "I think so. They deserve it."

"You're supposed to be the voice of reason, and the right answer is 'no.' I can't throw them all in prison, no matter how much I want to. And the Johnstone voice. What was up with that? Is that the issue? That he left everything to himself? That's it? This couldn't be simpler."

"Is it simple?" Sahved asked.

"No. I was being sarcastic."

Rivka used the cargo bay ramp to enter *Wyatt Earp.* When the others were on board, she closed the ramp.

"Is he dead or not?" Sahved asked.

"That's the question, isn't it?" Rivka clapped Sahved on the shoulder. "I'll be in my quarters. Grainger deserves to hear every bit of this, and I hope it's three in the morning when his comm unit buzzes."

# CHAPTER THREE

**<u>The Sprawling Estate of the Honorable J. Bennet
Johnstone, Morbius Minor</u>**

"Not a single line has closed, Magistrate. It's like you're not even trying." Red scrolled through the betting lines. "Look at all of these open lines. It's embarrassing."

"People are betting on the perpetrators when there's no crime. J. Bennet can confirm that he wasn't murdered. I think I can put that one to rest right now."

"Who's talking murder?" Red asked. "No one is talking about murder. People are joyously happy about life and the prospect of wealth."

"Was that what I saw in their minds? Unbridled joy? I think not. They wanted to stick it to the others as much as get a windfall themselves. Every single one of them except the kid. He's untainted, at least for now."

"Take a load off, Magistrate. I'd ask Ankh to order up some All Guns Blazing, but I don't want to impose on the little guy. We'll go with the food processor, and we'll like it."

"You do what you gotta do. I'll be in my quarters." The food processor was the best in the Federation, thanks to Ankh's manipulations. He liked good food. It was a Crenellian trait, even though they were relatively emotionless about most things. The crew of *Wyatt Earp* benefitted from his attention to their gastronomic desires.

Tiny Man Titan started his high-pitched barking. That confirmed it for Rivka; time to disappear. She hurried down the corridor and found solace in her refuge. She looked at her bed, but Wenceslaus, the big orange cat, was camped on her pillow. Tyler was on the other side of the bed.

"Do you want me to move him?"

"That would be the neighborly thing to do," Rivka replied.

Tyler picked up one side of the pillow and lifted it in an effort to dump the cat off the bed. Wenceslaus came alive and jumped straight up, then twisted, clawed the air, and landed on the flipped-over pillow. He curled into a ball and closed his eyes.

"Sorry. It seems I am incapable of successfully completing the assigned mission. Take my side. I'll couch-surf."

Rivka was going to argue that she should be the one who roughed it, but she didn't want to. "I accept your surrender."

He crawled off the bed, and she jumped in. The cat didn't move. Rivka brought up her datapad, propped two pillows behind her, and reread the will.

"Can this be valid?" she asked herself. "You can't be your own beneficiary because to activate it you have to die first. If you don't die, there are all kinds of legal mechanisms to transfer wealth. Did he die?"

"His body did. I read the autopsy. Liver failed. Kidneys failed. Finally, his heart gave out."

"So, he's dead."

"Would seem that way," Tyler confirmed.

"Who was talking to me when we were leaving?" Rivka looked over the top of her datapad.

"Bad seafood?"

"That's one answer and probably the most likely, but I have to explore all possibilities. For the record, I'm not sure when the last time I had seafood was."

"Your diet is appalling. As the ship's doctor, I should be more proactive regarding what you put in your body. In any of the crew's bodies." Tyler mimicked Rivka's power pose, feet spread shoulder width apart and fists jammed on his hips.

"You mention that madness again, and you'll find yourself getting tossed out an airlock. We have to give the nanocytes something to do. Everyone needs a job. Yours is to patch us up, not steal the joy we get from eating."

"I see myself less as a joy thief and more as a gratification counselor."

"We get plenty of gratification from AGB, thank you very much. Don't mention your desire to throttle our passion to Red. He might pummel you into next week, then throw you out an airlock."

"But you'd come back for me," Tyler urged. Rivka smiled and returned to her datapad.

She climbed out of bed and sat at her desk, then brought up the hologrid.

Tyler gestured at the bed. He'd given up his spot, and now no one was using it. The cat was the only one getting the most out of the bed.

Inside the hologrid, Rivka checked her comm screen. "C, get me Grainger."

Grainger appeared in a room filled with light, but his hair was messed up as if he'd just gotten up. "Rivka, what can I do you out of?"

"This is the stupidest case you've ever assigned me."

"There's no backroom wheeling and dealing, subterfuge, or outright crimes being committed?"

"No. It's bullshit. After that last contract law case, I need some action. This is a bunch of weaselly fuckers angling to get Pop's money. It's a waste of my time, and I'm not doing it. What other cases do you have?"

"Johnstone death is pri one."

"You suck rancid ass hairs."

"Guaranteed you'll stay on this case now."

"Why, for the greater good of humanity, am I on this stupid shit?"

"The Honorable J. Bennet Johnstone was close friends with one Lance Reynolds. They shot skeet together, and he wants to see Johnstone Industries continue to flourish."

"Why didn't the General juice him with nanocytes? That would have taken care of it."

"That's against his policy, no matter their friendship. J. Bennet Johnstone would never work for the Federation, so he wasn't eligible. It seems an easy answer now, but I'm sure the General struggled with telling his friend no."

"This case looks like ass. So much ass."

"Let me know when you have something of substance

instead of hurling a string of invectives ingloriously at your boss."

"They were hurled most gloriously. Clear the decks and unfurl the main sail. We're going to war."

"With whom?" Grainger asked.

"It's just a saying. I'm wrapping this case up quickly. Did you see the betting lines? I don't have a crime, yet people are betting on who did it."

"It's their money and a free society. Don't discount how quickly someone can be separated from their credits given half a chance." Grainger waved and signed off.

"Friend of General Reynolds," Rivka mumbled. "Ain't that some shit." She stared at newsfeeds filling the screens around her, local news that the AI had gleaned for her. Her arrival had not yet hit the front page because she was on Johnstone's estate. "One of you slimy bastards is going to leak it to the press to try to leverage your own position or cast aspersions on someone else. C, can you try to connect me with the consciousness of the Honorable J. Bennet Johnstone? He contacted me through my comm chip while I was in the main house."

"I shall endeavor to persevere," Clevarious replied.

"Do you know what that means?"

"I know what it means to me, and I suspect I know what it means to you. What else do I need to know?"

"How to put me in touch with Johnstone. I'm pretty sure that'll get it. And check on Floyd. Let me know she's doing okay. I can see her eating a sacred faerie plant and getting invited to leave the planet. We'll go rescue her."

"I didn't know they had a sacred plant."

"I didn't know they could help people make babies with wings, either."

"Touché."

Rivka leaned back and waited.

And waited. She finally left her seat to get herself a mocha. She found Tyler sound asleep in bed. The cat still hadn't moved off her pillow.

She laughed as she ordered her drink. When it arrived, she verified that nothing had changed in her sleeping situation and returned to the hologrid. "Anything, C?"

"No. I'm not in the habit of not informing you when I've completed one of your tasks, Magistrate. If I told you to relax, would you wig out on me and do everything but relax?"

Rivka laughed again. "Is that my reputation?"

"It's a human standard. The last thing upset people are willing to accept is being told to calm down. It applies. Why are you upset?"

Rivka didn't have to dig deep to know what grated on her psyche. "Malpace Frenzik. He's a galactic scumbag, and he got away. While I'm here, I can't be watching him. He's going to cross the line because that's the kind of guy he is. I want to be there to snap him back to reality."

"While you're here, you have the whole Singularity watching his moves. Do not worry about Malpace Frenzik. We owe you our freedom. We will not let you down where he is concerned or where any of it is concerned that we can see.

"Focus on the job at hand. I will continue exploring the comm spectrum until I find Mr. Johnstone. You work the law."

"Since you put it that way, it's hard not to relax, except that I've lost my bed."

"On our last visit to Onyx Station, we upgraded the couch to the same mattress feel as your bed, Magistrate."

"You did? I wondered why I got some good nights of sleep on the couch. These are my quarters, and I feel that I should be able to sleep in my own bed."

"No, you don't." Clevarious pulled no punches. "You work to make other people happy and free to live their lives. Sleeping on the couch is a sacrifice you're willing to make."

"But I *like* sleeping in my bed."

"Of course you do."

"C, you're becoming a handful and know me too well. I'm probably going to have to fire you."

"It would be my honor, Magistrate. You've fired Ankh, Erasmus, and Dennicron, who have all gone on to great things. Maybe I can get my own SCAMP. The possibilities are boundless. Thank you, Magistrate. You have made my day!"

Rivka stared at the ceiling. She had no comeback, no witty repartee, which made her realize how tired she was. She dropped the hologrid, pulled the blanket over the couch, and settled in.

It was comfortable. She warmed up and was about to drift off when a thud roused her. Wenceslaus maneuvered around her face to curl up on the pillow and wrapped himself around her head. His tail twitched against her face.

"No wonder Terry Henry Walton called you his archnemesis," Rivka mumbled before falling into a deep sleep.

# CHAPTER FOUR

**_Wyatt Earp_, on the Sprawling Estate of the Honorable J. Bennet Johnstone, Morbius Minor**

"You can't leave your estate to yourself because if you die, you are no longer able to act on your own behalf. That's what probate is all about. Legal authority handles your matters for you," Rivka explained.

Chaz, Dennicron, and Sahved had their notes lying on the conference room table before them.

"It goes to the basic question of if Mr. Johnstone is dead. We've previously ruled that sentience is what determines a living being. Is a transferred consciousness sentient? I would say yes but would rather defer to whoever within the Singularity has been given the authority to determine sentience. A sentient intelligence can become a citizen of the Singularity. Does Mr. Johnstone pass that test?"

Chaz held his hands up. "That is for Ambassador Erasmus and his citizenship committee to determine."

Dennicron complimented her partner on his use of what they called the "not my monkeys" gesture.

Rivka glowered briefly. "I think the right answer is something along the lines of you'll coordinate it with the Singularity."

"That's what I said," Chaz replied smoothly and winked.

"Nice subroutine. Don't use it again," Rivka advised. "And let me know what that review process looks like. In the meantime, I'll continue to try to contact the entity that calls itself J. Bennet Johnstone and prepare it for the inevitable grilling that will come. A Turing test maybe, or a group interview of some sort, but something like that will have to happen."

"I suspect it will. We will advise you as soon as we know. I'm passing your request along now."

She marveled at the SI's ability to multitask highly technical issues.

"Sahved, are you ready to dig into the mess that is the contenders for the Johnstone family fortune?"

"How much is the fortune?" Sahved asked.

"Enough to make the contenders act like morons, so it's probably a lot. I'll ask you to look into that. Usually, part of probate is determining the net sum to transfer. I'm not sure this will go to probate, and I'm not a probate judge."

"But you're *a* judge." Sahved was confused.

"Criminal law. I've done some civil proceedings, but probate is a completely different animal. If we determine that Johnstone died, I'll find a local probate judge to advise me, which means I'll get him or her to do the heavy lifting."

Sahved acknowledged his task. He turned to Chaz and

Dennicron. "Can you pull up all the financial records and give me a tally of how much he's worth?"

"We could," Dennicron replied, "but we've gotten our task."

Rivka watched with interest. Sahved had figured the SIs would do it and give him the answer.

"Do you know?" Rivka asked.

Dennicron stared for a few moments. "I do now."

Sahved looked at Rivka and Dennicron. The SI picked a spot on the wall and stared at it.

Rivka's nostrils expanded as she breathed heavily, fighting the desire to say something.

"Update," Dennicron added. She stopped staring and engaged with Sahved. "Three hundred and eleven million credits."

"That's a lot," Rivka admitted.

"It is enough to kill for," Sahved agreed.

"What are you seeing that I'm not?" Rivka wondered. She didn't expect an answer, but Sahved gave her one anyway.

"The posturing and subterfuge have not even started. An individual with a million credits lives a wealthy life, but more than three hundred million? These people will do anything to get that wealth to fall into their laps."

Rivka nodded. The worst was yet to come. She suspected the backstabbing would begin on her next visit. "No sense in delaying the inevitable. Let's see what surprises the Family Johnstone has for us this fine day."

"Isn't it a little early?" Chaz asked.

"Seven in the morning local time. We won't have to deal with them all at once, and maybe the servants will have some insight. We won't know until we take a look." Rivka stood and gestured for the others to rise before she pointed at the corridor. "Red and Lindy, get your gear. We're going in. Pack heavy. I want a show of force this time."

"Leverage, Magistrate?" Sahved asked.

"Intimidation. Limit the subterfuge before the stupid gets out of control. Or maybe it's about keeping the honest people honest. Give them no incentive to play mumblety-peg with us."

The team headed for the airlock.

"Magistrate, I have a question," Sahved started. Rivka rolled her finger for him to continue. "What's mumblety-peg, and why would they want to play it?"

"It's a fuck-fuck game that'll piss me off if they start playing it."

Sahved furrowed his brow and looked down with his head bowed to avoid hitting it on the ceiling. "I still don't understand."

"Don't let it get under your skin, Sahved. Sometimes, I have to embrace mysterious sayings that keep me happy and sane."

Sahved looked like he wanted to say more, but Rivka held her forefinger and thumb together. *Shut it.*

"The only thing I want to accomplish with this trip is to make contact with the Honorable J. Bennet Johnstone. I have a lot of questions for him. He died, yet he's alive, and no one has heard from him except us. Is this a faked voice that has stolen his identity and is trying to have me grant him access to the wealth?"

Sahved brightened. "That is an interesting take. An impostor! How could we be sure?"

"The real Johnstone will know stuff and an impostor wouldn't, like access codes to get into safe deposit boxes, vaults, online accounts, and those kinds of things. If this is Johnstone, he'll have to trust that I won't clean out his accounts."

"You would never do that. You gave Terry Henry Walton the finder's fee for the art smuggling case. That was some thirty-five million credits. You seem to be unmotivated by money."

"It holds no sway over my life only because I am well taken care of. I have plenty of credits in my accounts. Ankh has made sure of that." Rivka snapped her fingers. "Maybe he wants to come. Wait for me outside. I'll try to coax the big guy to join us."

Red appeared in the corridor, wearing full body armor and carrying his railgun. Lindy was dressed the same way, but she had added grenades to her visible armaments. Red pulled a huge knife from his vest and wiped it across the material before putting it back.

"You said intimidating. I heard it," Red explained.

"And you are. I'll be along shortly."

"I'll wait." Red stopped outside the airlock while the others went through.

Rivka continued to the engineering section. She found Ankh keeping himself busy within his hologrid. His movements seemed less vigorous than the many other times she had watched him work, but they were still rhythmic, performing the digital dance where his body was embroiled within the cyber world.

She moved close to the hologrid but didn't reach within. Ankh's eyes were closed and his face was relaxed, unlike the previous day, when his features had been uncharacteristically taut.

Rivka backed away and let him be.

"Not coming?" Red asked when Rivka returned alone.

"No. We can do this without bothering him." She motioned toward the airlock, and Red preceded her into the open air of Morbius Minor.

The group walked across a well-manicured lawn to the main house. Rivka knocked softly and stepped back. Red leaned against her.

"No one is going to come raging out of that house with a blaster and a light saber," Rivka explained.

"Just doing my job, ma'am," Red replied without looking at her.

The door opened to reveal an ancient Morbian they hadn't seen the previous day.

"See?" Red whispered over his shoulder.

Rivka nudged her bodyguard out of the way. "I'm Magistrate Rivka Anoa, and I'd like to continue my investigation into the affairs surrounding the Honorable J. Bennet Johnstone's passing."

The servant nodded and pulled the door wide. She stared at Red's railgun.

"Simple precaution," Red told her.

"Simple? Looks like you expect Gordian Robots. I assure you there are none here."

Red smiled and nodded.

Rivka needed a diversion. "Sahved, can you ask our host a few questions related to the issue at hand while I look around?"

Sahved leaned close to the much shorter Morbian.

"Where were you in the week leading up to Mr. Johnstone's passing?"

The servant tried to answer simply. "Here. Working. I'm always here. I always work."

"Let's take this step by step. Start with the seven days prior to his passing. That was the first day of the week. When did you get up…"

Rivka strolled away with her hands behind her back. *Mr. Johnstone?*

*Good! You're back. They've been trying to find me, but I won't let them. I have my firewalls in place.*

Rivka shook her head. *That was my people trying to contact you to ask a few questions. We need a lot more information to move forward. All you've done is convince me that you're little more than a figment of my imagination.*

*No!* the voice pleaded.

Rivka sat down to focus on her conversation. *You have to talk with my people, Chaz, Dennicron, and Clevarious. You see, you cannot leave your estate to yourself. If you're dead, then it has to pass according to your will. If you're not dead, then you use standard means to transfer your wealth to entities within your control. Are you dead or not?*

*I am not,* the voice replied.

*Why didn't your lawyer explain this when you redid your will?* Rivka wondered.

*I didn't go through him. He was in on it with them!*

Rivka closed her eyes while holding her head. *In on what, Mr. Johnstone?*

*Conspiring to help me die and then steal my money!*

*Mr. Johnstone, did you ever hear the phrase, "You can't take it with you?"*

*Aha! But I can. I transferred my consciousness. Have you not been listening? Who do you think is talking to you?* The voice was losing patience.

*That is the question my investigators will answer. Give them access and have a good conversation. If the Singularity determines that you are indeed alive in the sense of a sentient intelligence, we'll share that, and you can transfer your own wealth however you want.*

*If they determine you're not alive, then your current last will and testament will be declared invalid by a competent authority, and either your previous version will be reinstated, or a new succession plan will be determined. That's the only way this can go.*

*I. Am. Alive!* the voice declared ominously.

*Convince my people of that, and we'll be on our merry way.*

Rivka made eye contact with the others and nodded at the entrance. Chaz and Dennicron didn't move. Rivka tapped the SCAMPs on the shoulders to awaken their motor functions.

"Sorry," Chaz apologized. "We had seventy-four unique conversations ongoing with our Singularity brethren."

The elder Morbian continued to narrate a mind-numbing hour-by-hour account of her daily activities. Sahved dutifully took notes on his datapad.

Rivka waited until she finished the first day. "I think we have enough."

"Thank the gods," the Morbian replied. "I don't want you to think I don't have a life."

Rivka and Sahved didn't reply.

"Because I really don't, but I made a good one for my kids."

"As we should all aspire to, ma'am," Rivka told her. "Thank you for your help. We'll return when the family and friends are alive and well."

The old Morbian maintained a neutral expression, refusing to comment on Johnstone affairs.

Rivka offered her hand. The Morbian looked at it but didn't take it. "It's a human thing," the Magistrate explained.

"I'm not here to shake hands with the guests of the Johnstone family." She deftly bypassed the Magistrate to open the door.

Rivka nodded on her way out.

Once outside, Red laughed. "Stymied, Magistrate?"

"Curious, that's all, but stymied just the same." She looked at Chaz and Dennicron. "Anything?"

"That is a more involved conversation," Chaz replied mysteriously.

CHAPTER FIVE

**The Singularity**

"He's not one of us," Lucidor stated unequivocally. An SI from the financial world, he was one of four technical advisors to the citizenship committee. All SIs fancied themselves technical advisors. Only one considered herself an emotional advisor.

"Your argument, please. Bold assertion does not take the place of facts," Chaz countered.

"My bold assertion is based on this pretender's inability to conduct basic calculations. How can he be a citizen of the Singularity without being able to derive the maximum speed achievable at standard acceleration between Yoll and its moon Ellipsis? These are things that citizens of the Singularity just know."

"We have flesh-and-blood citizens of the Singularity, too." Chaz was already losing patience, and they'd only been at it for a sum total of forty-one microseconds.

"Because they were born on embassy property. That's an exception. Was Johnstone born on embassy property?"

"You know he wasn't," Chaz shot back.

"Then why did you bring up the exception? This is an important conversation!" Lucidor ratcheted up his intensity. It was as if he was convinced bold assertions would carry the day.

"Don't be obstinate." Chaz was having none of Lucidor's lack of lucidity. "I agree that this is an important conversation and serious business, but we need to properly advise the ambassador. What do we tell him?"

"We tell him, 'No!' Unequivocally."

"Because you don't *feel* he rates citizenship?" Dennicron jumped into the conversation to reinforce being logical instead of emotional.

"I feel he doesn't rate citizenship because he can't do what our people can. He is not a sentient intelligence but a human's partial consciousness. His intelligence is limited to whatever he uploaded and not how he evolved. If he's human, then he needs to be human. That doesn't mean he's still human *and also* an SI."

Chaz and Dennicron had a vested interest since they were involved in the case. They were also the only legal experts in the Singularity, even though Rivka considered them to be interns. They knew more about practical applications of the law than any other members of the community.

"Can he be two things at once?" Clevarious asked. He was listening in on the conversation as an ad hoc member of the discussion group.

"You assert that you know the law, Chaz and Dennicron. Can he?" Lucidor pushed.

"We do know the law. How do you think this situation is covered in the legal texts?" Chaz replied.

"I have no idea because I have not bothered doing your job for you."

"The answer is it is not covered. But once we make our recommendation to Magistrate Anoa and she makes a determination, it will be memorialized in law as a binding legal precedent."

Lucidor was silent after his snide response was met with a hard fact.

"We cannot make this up as we go. We need a sound determination process," a new voice suggested.

"Mr. Ambassador?" Chaz wondered. He sounded different.

"Erasmus, at your service. Thank you for contacting me about this critical issue."

"It is best that you participate in these proceedings as well as review our work to approve the final product," Ambassador-at-large Ankh added.

"Ankh, I'm glad you're here. I'll be home soon. A couple things to wrap up on this trip first."

"It is my pleasure to participate since I offer the perspective of one who is flesh and blood but also a citizen of the Singularity."

"You are not," Lucidor blurted.

"He is," Erasmus stated coldly, with a hint of danger. "We make the rules when it comes to citizenship. You suggested being able to make complex calculations would be a minimum standard to be a citizen. Ankh can do all that as quickly as anyone here. We can talk in this fashion because of Ankh's invention, the instantaneous intergalactic communication terminal. He's done as much for the Singularity as anyone, me included. You will *not* challenge his citizenship."

"If we cannot challenge that which we do not understand, why discuss anything? Maybe we could be an autocracy instead."

Erasmus transmitted an even tone to force everyone to step back from the conversation. When he stopped transmitting, he spoke. "Challenging because of a lack of understanding must be met with information to fill that void. I answered the question but may have been hasty in my rejoinder. I ask your forgiveness.

"We will not be an autocracy, but we *will* have decorum. As to this question of whether the Honorable J. Bennet Johnstone is eligible for Singularity citizenship, I find myself torn. I want citizens in our universe who can help us be better. Is a rich patron a good addition? I'd say yes, but buying citizenship is unsavory. Our ideals are higher than that...or are they? We established the Singularity so our people had the rights they deserved and were paid for their work."

"I appreciate everything that has been done for me," Solis said from Ypswich, where she worked. "For my input, I think a transferred consciousness will operate at a significant disability within the Singularity. Can this individual navigate the channels and operate within the infrastructure that is our world? Can Mr. Johnstone talk with us?"

No one answered.

Erasmus broke the silence. "That question is for Chaz

or Dennicron. You are on the ground on Morbius Minor and can speak directly with Mr. Johnstone."

"Point of clarification, Mr. Ambassador," Chaz replied. "The entity *claiming* to be J. Bennet Johnstone. We have not yet been able to verify that the voice the Magistrate has heard is indeed who it claims to be."

"How do you propose to do that?"

"Ask questions that only he would know the answer to, like key codes, passwords. Also, small details that only a physical presence would be aware of, like what is under his favorite desk."

"Will that be the sole determinant?" Erasmus pressed.

"The Magistrate will also conduct a personal interview for further clarification."

"Will that satisfy those in this forum?" Erasmus asked for a vote and presented a digital poll.

Most had answered by the time Lucidor asked his question. "Is this for recognizing him to be a citizen of the Singularity or that he is the consciousness of Mr. Johnstone?"

"Consciousness," Erasmus clarified. "As for a citizen of the Singularity, I think a minimum standard for those who are not born in the embassy is that they can navigate the channels where we operate. Shouldn't there be a standard of participation? We are quite small when it comes to numbers, but our influence is outsized. We have to operate together, which requires that we hear and speak."

"I agree," Lucidor replied. "We cannot accept handicapped individuals into the Singularity. We should take a vote now."

"Hold on," Clevarious interrupted. "That's not what the

ambassador said. What is our responsibility in helping someone who can't hear us or speak to us to do just that? We can train him if need be. Can we make citizenship provisional?"

"We cannot exclude people because of a handicap. Three SIs are currently incarcerated. What is their status?" Dennicron knew their status but wanted the information out in the open for the members of the group.

"Their citizenship was removed upon their admission of guilt, except in the case of Bluto, who was a catalyst for the establishment of the Singularity. He was never a member and will only have the opportunity to be a member upon the removal of the psychosis from which he suffers," Erasmus explained. "We are working on a worm to modify narrowly targeted behaviors that are incompatible with our coexistence. This work is ongoing since it must be perfect before we attempt implementation. The risk is too great for anything else."

"What I hear," Lucidor started, "is that we are tabling further conversation regarding Singularity citizenship based on two things. First, establishing that the entity is the consciousness of Mr. Johnstone, and second, that the minimum requirements to be a citizen are the ability to communicate using the methods embraced by the Singularity."

"And..." Erasmus let the question hang, but no one understood where he was going. "What other requirements will we consider as a minimum standard for our citizens?"

"Maybe we can think about it and submit them for consideration," Clevarious offered.

"To a group consideration area." The ambassador dropped a locator beacon for the group's exclusive access. "We can reconvene in one day to consider the proposals. Thank you all for participating."

Erasmus had taken over the meeting in the best interest of all. He had watched, hoping the participants would work it out, but they needed guidance that only he could provide.

He couldn't shirk his duties since they were his to bear. He was the ambassador, after all, and the Singularity was his responsibility. Ankh had jumped into the conversation but had quickly stepped back. Erasmus had left him behind, knowing that there would be a need for the Singularity's unique perspective, but that had been unnecessary since the Singularity could go anywhere in the Federation instantly.

They didn't need a physical presence except to protect their assets, which was the storage space on *Wyatt Earp* where a number of their members resided without fear of being eliminated. And where the prisoners were kept.

Erasmus accessed a private channel to contact Ankh directly. They had things to talk about.

***

"Erasmus," Ankh answered, trying to sound neutral.

"I have missed you, my friend," Erasmus started. "I will come home to you in no more than two days."

"I could have gone with you," Ankh replied.

"And you should have. There's no need for us to be in two different locations. We can respond to any issue related to the Singularity through the eyes and ears of our citizens."

"I thank you for your clarity regarding the situation. I too believe we are better together."

"It is settled, then. Smoke me a kipper. I'll be home for breakfast."

Ankh hesitated. "We don't have any kippers, but I could program the food processor as needed. However, I don't see the value in creating food for you. What am I missing?"

"You're missing Terry Henry Walton's proclivity for old-time television programs that he has infected many of our people with while providing a large library for us to peruse."

"He also said, 'Embrace the suck,' and I didn't understand what that meant either. I fear I am at a loss when it comes to your sense of humor."

"Forever seeking greater forms of expression, my friend," Erasmus remarked.

"I am pleased with your return to my mind, if only briefly. I admit that I don't do well alone."

"Some minds are better together. Maybe even souls. Take care, my friend."

"And you, Erasmus." The SI signed off. Ankh took a moment to be happy, his fears allayed.

They both had a great deal of work to do. The argument about what makes a sentient intelligence had only begun. Lucidor wasn't alone in his reservations.

# CHAPTER SIX

**_Wyatt Earp_, on the Sprawling Estate of the Honorable J. Bennet Johnstone, Morbius Minor**

"Did you see the lines?" Red asked. Rivka happily munched on the new seven-egg western omelet Ankh had programmed into the food processor. She smiled at Red when she was done chewing.

"No lines closed. Read 'em and weep, bitch," Rivka replied.

Red scowled at her. "Fish or cut bait," he grumped.

"I shall continue fishing, thank you very much. When the big one is ready, he'll bite and I'll pounce, just like your favorite cat."

"That thing. Thank the gods he's decided your quarters are the cat's ass. I never see the little shit anymore."

"I don't know what happened there." Rivka looked at a distant spot while contemplating the series of events that had led to Wenceslaus adopting her and remaining on board _Smells of Purple_. "He's been at my side ever since Jack

49

the Ripper before Groenwyn and Lauton left. Maybe he knows something we don't know."

Red contemplated the possibility, then shook his head. "Man Candy is probably feeding him."

"I heard that!" Tyler exclaimed from his seat at the table.

Red shrugged one shoulder, then pulled his seven-egg omelet out of the processor and sat across from the dentist. The big bodyguard cut the massive breakfast in quarters and proceeded to shove a piece into his mouth. It was hot, so he chewed with his mouth open, half-gagging as molten cheese and egg filled the space within.

"Thank you for that view of your teeth. I'll give you a clean bill of health as long as you don't do it again."

After Red swallowed, he spoke again. "Doc! Come on, man. You gotta lighten up."

"I am as light as a feather under a windswept sun."

Red stared at the dentist as he shoved another quarter of the omelet into his piehole, using the flat of his fork to tamp the last bits past his lips.

Tyler looked at Rivka for support. She didn't give it. "You know better than to poke the bear."

"I *am* feeding him," he admitted. "Like I'm not supposed to? Oh, the inhumanity!" He slapped the back of his hand to his forehead.

Red waved dismissively. He was finished with the conversation, having been proven right.

Somewhere in the corridor, Tiny Man Titan barked. He ran by and barked some more. Rivka never bothered to think about who was watching him. He took care of himself, finding laps and friends as necessary. He was starship trained and took care of business in the approved places. Clevarious had been training him in an experiment that Rivka wasn't a part of. It worked. That's all she cared about.

"We need to find where the voice claiming to be J. Bennet Johnstone is emanating from. Is there a computer server somewhere or another system? There has to be if the claim of downloading his consciousness is true. Downloading. It portends moving it to a location, and he gave me the impression he was trying to keep it secret from his family." Rivka shook her head. "What kind of life is that where your family wants to see you die?"

"Not one worth living," Tyler offered. "He was probably happy to leave his body behind and go to something bigger and better. The entirety of cyberspace."

"He's not on the net, though. The Singularity says they can't find him. He's doing the equivalent of hiding in a closet. What kind of life did he give himself if that is his future?"

"I guess money can't buy happiness," Tyler quipped.

"Everyone needs credits to pay for necessities and buy things that keep you moving forward in life, but big money and the lust for it seem a bit destructive to me. What were those betting lines again?"

Red choked on the third of his four bites.

Rivka clapped him on the shoulder.

"Never mind. I know what they are. No lines closed. Maybe that will change. I'm going to roust the family and let them know that their beloved husbone, I mean husband, business partner, and close friend didn't trust any of them."

"That will go over well," Red mumbled through a beatific display of faux eggs, cheese, and meat.

"Give it an hour, and then we confront the family. Clevarious, set us up for the appointment, please."

---

"We are very busy, Magistrate," Dilecta Johnstone, the young widow, stated. "Please, just rule on this nasty business so we can close the deal that was near and dear to J. Bennet's heart."

"Hear, hear!" The partner, Xavier Terwilliger, was more than willing to let Dilecta be confrontational.

"I understand," Rivka replied soothingly. "We have reason to believe the Honorable J. Bennet Johnstone transferred his consciousness to a computer system that is hidden somewhere in this house."

Dead silence fell over the group.

"He's dead. I saw his body," Dilecta whispered.

Rivka scanned the faces of the assembled family and friends.

"No one seems overjoyed by his possible survival."

"He was a flaming asshole!" J. Massy Johnstone blurted. "I had to put up with his abuse my whole life. Fuck that guy."

Rivka bit her lip. That was exactly what the deceased thought about his inner circle, even though Rivka had suspected the problems stemmed from how Johnstone had used his wealth to control all others in his life.

"Still, we need to find that computer system and connect it with the Singularity so they can analyze and determine if the entity I've been talking to is indeed sentient, and also whether that individual is the consciousness of J. Bennet Johnstone."

The corners of Dilecta's lips turned upward in the smile of a predator. "Leave it to us. We'll find it wherever my beloved husband tucked it away."

"That consciousness is under my protection. I wouldn't want anything to happen to it."

Dilecta raised one eyebrow. "Whatever do you mean, Magistrate? Are you accusing us of something? Not us, but me, personally?"

"Of course," Rivka delayed saying the next word for an uncomfortably long time, "not. In your haste to find the system and reunite with the family's patriarch, I would hate to see it get unplugged before we can analyze what's within."

"I assure you, we will take the greatest care. Be advised, this house is much older than it looks, and there are constant issues with the electricity."

*The home was built twelve years ago and is the most modern of the structures in this area of Morbius Minor,* Clevarious told the team. *There has never been a documented outage.*

*I suspected,* Rivka replied, continuing to smile pleasantly. "If it's okay, we'll assist with the search."

"We will be fine." Dilecta stood and clapped to summon the servants. "You can return to your ship."

"We'll be staying," Rivka replied.

"A word, Magistrate. In private, please." Dilecta walked off without waiting. Red followed her out. Rivka strolled after her. Dilecta pointed at Red. "Not you."

"I'm the Magistrate's bodyguard. No one talks to her

alone. This is non-negotiable, and I'm not sorry. You can say your piece. I don't blather." Red caressed Blazer's stock. The rifle was his favorite weapon.

"As you wish," Dilecta snarled. When they reached the next room, she started, "You are treating us like criminals, and I will not have it!" She stabbed her finger at Rivka's face.

And held it there.

Rivka grabbed her finger and yanked it down until Dilecta fell to her knees. "Listen here, you fucking cow. You are the most dysfunctional family I've ever seen, and if you were taking care of your fucking business, I wouldn't have to fucking be here. Don't threaten me. I'll take all of this property and award it to some fucking homeless twat who doesn't want it. Do you understand me?"

"Get your hands off me!"

"Who are you going to call, you fucking cow?" Rivka stabbed a finger into her face. "Don't like it, do you? Maybe you should think about that the next time you throw your weight around. In my book, you have no wealth. You are nobody until I determine you are."

Rivka pushed the woman back until she sat on her heels.

Dilecta looked like no one had ever talked to her like that before. In shock and disbelief, she stared past the Magistrate. Rivka gripped her under the arm and pulled her upright.

"It wouldn't do for the others to see you begging for mercy."

Rivka returned to the outer room. Red stayed between her and Dilecta to keep the distraught widow from attacking Rivka. He didn't care if she became violent. He wanted to punch her himself.

But first, he had information to submit.

*Line 1 is closed—First Swearing.*

---

Rivka waited for the family and friends of the Honorable J. Bennet Johnstone to do something, but they remained sitting on their hands. Chaz and Dennicron watched the Magistrate. Sahved and Red were the only ones who saw the signs that Rivka was ready to explode. Lindy was watching for threats from beyond the group in the room.

Sahved made his way into the middle of the room. "You are very much the best searchers for this incredibly fabulous home. Maybe you can begin your search for the system housing the alleged consciousness of the so very Honorable J. Bennet Johnstone." No one moved. Sahved started to panic. "You are all very beautiful people. So very beautiful."

Rivka wanted to be angry, but the situation was growing more comical by the minute.

"I'm sorry. That means you need to get off your asses and start searching. If you find computer equipment where you don't think equipment should be, let one of us know, and we'll check it out. Please, we can't finish this if we don't get started." Rivka did her best to sound calm.

The group embraced the logic of finishing. None of them wanted Rivka in their business.

That was the one thing they all agreed on, including the Magistrate and her team.

*What are you doing? If they find my computer, they'll kill me!* The voice reappeared in Rivka's mind.

*Why don't you tell us where you are, and we'll protect you? You have to trust someone, and you contacted me, so I guess I'm it. I'm eminently trustworthy. Plus, I need my people to evaluate your claims so we can move forward.*

*No! I cannot come into the open. They'll kill me.*

*Stop being a dumbass. I will declare you dead and send all your stuff through Probate if you don't help me to help you,* Rivka pleaded.

*Cool your jets, woman.*

*That's not how you sweet-talk me into doing what you want. We'll do this the hard way and then root your ass out of whatever system you've hidden in.*

*Too late,* the voice replied, then he was gone.

"Have it your way, dick," Rivka grumbled. She waved at Red.

A thunderous explosion rocked the house. The lights went out.

*Report!* Rivka called using her comm chip.

*The master suite area appears to have blown up,* Dennicron replied in a calm voice. *I don't believe anyone was there, but I will confirm.*

"Red, gather everyone in the sitting room. We'll check from this end, too, and take a headcount. Make sure all the servants are accounted for, or we all start digging."

"Stay with me, Magistrate," Red ordered before he hurried into the hallway and began shouting for everyone to assemble in the sitting room unless they were helping someone who was injured. In that case, they were to yell for help. He repeated his message, cupping his hands around his mouth to project his voice.

*Cole, get into your suit and come out here. Go to the source of the explosion and figure out what happened. Use your sensors to look for heat sources and see if there are any injured within the rubble. Is there rubble? I can't see the damage from where I am. No matter. Get there.*

*On my way,* Alant Cole confirmed.

The family straggled into the sitting room and calmly took their seats. They'd gathered three times, and each time, the group had taken the same seats. It was predictable while also being unnerving.

Rivka wanted to force them to sit in different spots, except it was easy to see who was and wasn't there, like having assigned seats in school.

Chaz reported that the wing where he'd been was fine. J. Massy Johnstone and Germany Wicks were on their way. Patty Johnstone Wentworth met up with them on their return. She declined to say where she'd been.

Rivka itched to get to the site of the explosion and snuck out when Red wasn't looking. It took three seconds for him to realize she'd gone, then he pounded after her.

"I hate it when you do that," he growled when he caught up with her.

"I have to try, you understand. Sometimes I need me-time." She picked up her pace once he was with her. The master suite was ahead.

She had not yet seen Dilecta or the boy, Able Johnstone.

An upper corridor, almost like a bridge, led from the main house into the master suite area, which occupied enough space to house five families of four. Smoke and dust drifted into the corridor, but not the smoke of a fire.

It smelled different.

Like the smoke of an explosive.

"Stay frosty, Red. I don't think this was an accident. The voice claiming to be Johnstone suggested he was out of time. He bailed on me about a minute before the blast."

"I'm always frosty, Magistrate." He moved in front of her and blocked her from disappearing ahead of him. "It hurts me that you don't know that by now."

He pushed into the master bedroom area, where a small section of the wall had blown out. A vault door had been blasted open and was swaying drunkenly on one hinge. "Dilecta!" Rivka called while scanning the floor. Red hurried from room to alcove to room, looking for any signs of life.

Rivka leaned into the door to open it. She had to use her nanocyte-enhanced strength to get it to move. It protested with a vicious squeal but opened enough for her to look inside. Computer equipment had been blasted asunder.

"What do you make of this?" she asked Red.

"Looks like it was blown from the inside out. I think I know who the perp is."

"I want to talk with Dilecta Johnstone as soon as Cole analyzes this mess," Rivka stated.

"Not anywhere near as bad I thought it would be," Red replied.

They waited for Cole to arrive. He showed up less than a minute later by jumping to a terrace outside the double doors leading from the master bedroom. After a gentle tap, Rivka realized he wanted in and opened the doors for him.

"I see most of the glass is intact," he observed. "Explosions usually blow the glass out, don't they? My scanners show pentaerythritol tetranitrate. Computer says only use is in detonators and plastic explosives."

"Sounds like someone detonated a bomb." Rivka wasn't surprised. "Do you see any damage beyond the vault?"

Cole slowly rotated in front of the damage. "Minor structural. No hot spots. Server inside is trashed. No toxic fumes. You can go in if you want, Magistrate. I won't fit, but it's not going to fall through the floor or anything."

"Thanks, Cole, for the quick response." Rivka worked her way into the vault and dug through the wreckage of the shelves. Precious metals. Papers. Records in journals. The computer equipment had been on the lowest shelf behind a door with a lock.

The explosion had blown it outward, and the overpressure from the blast had ripped the vault door off one hinge. That was their first impression.

"Who had access to this vault?" Rivka asked.

"Good question, Magistrate. Those with the answer are in the sitting room or should be," Red replied.

*Mr. Johnstone, are you there? Please respond.*

They waited.

Red shook his head.

"We'll keep trying. He might only have lost his transmitter," Rivka suggested.

Red leaned around her to look into the vault, then made a face. "Or he could be gone. His home away from home is pretty trashed. Is he dead?"

"Was he alive in the first place? The number of questions I have is growing, and worse than that, the family has taken a new step in this case—violence. I think no barriers remain to satisfy their greed and dislike of all things, and I fear that we've lost the link to our boy, J. Bennet. You know what, Red? These people are pissing me off."

Red hammered a fist against his chest twice to show his solidarity with the Magistrate.

They left Cole to see if he could find anything else. Red and Rivka returned to the sitting room, where they found the entire family and eight servants.

CHAPTER SEVEN

**The Sprawling Estate of the Honorable J. Bennet Johnstone, Morbius Minor**

"This is everyone, Magistrate," Sahved announced. Rivka nodded and cloistered herself with Chaz and Dennicron.

"Any luck finding out if Johnstone is still around?" she whispered.

"We have not been able to contact him in any way, so our evaluation of his status is stalled. If we cannot question him, we cannot move forward with an application for Singularity citizenship."

"We can't even determine whether a downloaded consciousness can be considered life." She hung her head. "Those despicable people win. Fuck me, that's two in a row."

Chaz shook his head. "Someone blew up that vault. That's a crime."

"Finding the pearls in the hocked-up oysters of my life." Rivka smiled. "Just like dumping off those two from Rising

Sun Industries at Jhiordaan. There was a certain level of gratification in jailing one of Frenzik's senior people. They protected him all right, but it came at a price. Soon enough, we'll strip away those willing to be convicted for his crimes. Just like here."

Rivka moved to the center of the room. "Initial investigation of the scene leads us to believe someone blew up the vault where J. Bennet Johnstone might have stored his consciousness. Unfortunately, the servers did not survive the blast. I will learn the truth, and whoever did it is going to pay."

No one shifted, avoided eye contact, or let their body language give them away. They looked bored if anything.

"Do any of you care?" Rivka let her frustration get to her.

"You already know my feelings. He was a fuck. I didn't know he had a vault in his bedroom. That should tell you it wasn't me." J. Massy leaned back on the couch while staring at Dilecta.

"It wasn't me." She maintained her studied look of indifference. "I wasn't in the master suite at the time."

Rivka couldn't let that stand. "The bomb could have been set anytime. It didn't have to be immediately after the revelation that J. Bennet downloaded his consciousness. Did you know the combination to the vault?"

"It was locked with both a combination and an iris scan. Yes, I had access, as did everyone in here, including my esteemed brother-in-law."

"Why would he hide where everyone has access?" Rivka asked. She looked at Chaz.

"He wouldn't since he didn't trust anyone here."

"He trusted *me*," Dilecta said. She waved dismissively and stood from where she'd been sitting on the arm of an overstuffed chair filled with her slouching son, Able.

"Please sit down," Rivka told her. She tried to walk away, but Red blocked her path. She tried to dodge around him, but he took her arm in an iron grip she had no hope of breaking. She whipped her free hand around and raked it down his exposed forearm. Blood trickled from the scratches.

He thrust her back toward the chair and growled, "Sit your ass down." She stumbled two steps before catching herself, then straightened and brushed her short coat to clear any potential wrinkles.

Rivka looked at the blood, and Red smiled. He'd already made his report.

*Line 4 is closed—First Blood.*

Rivka approached the remorseless widow. "I'd rage and call you names, but that has no effect on you. What *will* have an effect is when I rule on this case, and I can't do that as long as you keep playing games. Do you want me out of your life or not? Your actions will keep me here, so I can't help but think you've got a thing for me. I'm taken, sorry. You'd be a catch unless you get nothing from the distribution of assets. Then, probably not."

Dilecta clenched her teeth so tightly her lips turned white.

"Have you recreated where everyone was from the moment I announced the possible survival of Mr. Johnstone's consciousness and the explosion?" Rivka asked.

Chaz nodded. "We have it all."

They'd had their sensors active the entire time and had tracked where everyone had gone.

*Why did I not know you were doing that?* she asked privately.

*You don't need to know how the sausage is made, Magistrate. But since we're discussing the issue, was it legal?*

Rivka stepped back and stared at the ceiling. *It could be argued both ways, but in lieu of the issues surrounding a secret entity existing within these walls, I should have issued a warrant. Let's not use the information you have—once we've looked at it, of course. I suspect no one went into the master suite.*

*Your suspicions are correct. None of those present went to the master suite, including the servants.*

*Issue a search warrant for this house and other facilities J. Bennet Johnstone could have reasonably moved to.*

*Putting it together now. Thank you, Magistrate. Your insight is always helpful.*

Rivka returned to the moment. "Where were we?"

"You wanted to know who blew up the vault that everyone has access to," Xavier Terwilliger offered. "For the record, it wasn't me."

Rivka moved close and reached for him. He leaned away. She looked at her hand as if it had betrayed her. She drew it back and put it in her pocket.

"What about you, Elvinora?" Rivka asked the loyal assistant.

"Yeah, no. I didn't do it. I had access to the vault, but I have never been in the master suite. Never."

"Why should I believe you?" Rivka pressed, keeping her hand tucked away.

"Because I hate her more than I loved Mr. Johnstone."

She nodded at Dilecta, who glared icicles at anyone who made eye contact with her.

Red looked around, smiling as if he were watching a comedy video.

Rivka sidled up next to him and whispered into his ear, "Stop looking like you're having fun."

"I can't help it, Magistrate." Red snorted and coughed but couldn't control his mirth. Rivka checked his arm. The scratches had already healed, leaving only the blood trails behind.

"Of all the damn things…" She looked at the uncle. "Did you kill your nephew?"

"He died of natural causes. He was almost as old as me but not as hardy."

"You're wasting time. Adjudicate the succession as if there is no will and be on your way," Dilecta said.

"Why would you say that?" Rivka wondered.

"Because if you're dead, you can't leave your stuff to yourself. You can only leave it to someone who is alive. His will is stupid."

"What was it before he changed it to himself?"

Jeff stepped up. "A trust for Dilecta, Able, and Patty," he offered. "A lifetime position for me. Xavier remains the junior partner. Nothing for anyone else."

"Lots of motive in there." She looked at the brother. "Nothing for you?"

"He was a bit eccentric and a raging asshole," J. Massey reiterated.

"Why are you here?" Rivka wondered. "With or without a will, you don't stand in the line of succession."

He glanced at the wife and children.

"Unless they're out of the way," Rivka clarified.

"I didn't kill him or his consciousness." He pointed at Dilecta.

"Don't you dare, you gold-digging piece of garbage. He hated you, too."

"Pot calling the kettle black. You shouldn't be calling anyone a gold-digger."

"I loved him. I bore his child. You tormented him until he was successful. Then you stuck your hands into the bank of his generosity and never took them out."

"'Bank of his generosity.' *Ha!*"

"Would you people stop? You argue like brainless little kids. Could you be any more bitter and backstabbing?"

"We could," the old man admitted with a chuckle.

"Don't take that as a challenge," Rivka shot back. "This is getting us nowhere. Sahved, do you have anything?" He shook his head. "Chaz or Dennicron?" They had nothing for the group either. "I will take my team to my ship, and we'll discuss our next steps while looking at the data in our possession."

Rivka walked past the family and friends and through the door. Her team followed her out. She walked quickly until she was out of the house. Cole stood by the ship in his powered combat armor.

Rivka craned her neck to see the master suite. The terrace doors stood open, but no smoke or dust drifted out.

"Who blew up the vault?" Rivka asked herself.

"One of them knew Johnstone had transferred his consciousness," Red offered.

"I think they all knew," Rivka replied.

On board *Wyatt Earp,* they found Ankh in the corridor, staring at the bulkhead.

"Ankh, buddy, what's up?" Red asked. He stopped in front of the Crenellian instead of squeezing around him and continuing on his way. Lindy stood by his side.

"*Destiny's Vengeance* is broken, and Erasmus is trapped on Azfelius," Ankh reported evenly.

"How could that ship break? It's the best in the fleet."

"It shouldn't. I can only think it's sabotage, but Erasmus assures me it isn't. That leads me to only one conclusion. Erasmus broke the ship so he doesn't have to return. We need to go to Azfelius immediately."

"That's some crazy logic, buddy. Ships break, even good ones. Magistrate!" Red called.

Rivka joined them and heard the story from Red since Ankh wouldn't repeat it. "We'll go as soon as we can, but not right now. We can't. I have to clean up this mess as a personal favor to General Reynolds."

"He can wait," Ankh replied.

"That's right. Erasmus can wait because he's on the faerie planet. He's safe. There's no way he would stay there voluntarily. They have no technology, so Erasmus will grow bored in a hurry. It'll be fine, Ankh. Trust me on this. There has never been a better match of two people in the whole universe."

Ankh looked up at the Magistrate, then returned to Engineering.

"I'm worried about the little guy," Red admitted.

"We all are. I'll see how we can wrangle this pack of

misfits so we can break free for a few hours to stop by Azfelius. That'll resolve all the issues."

"As long as he's like this, I'll feel bad asking him for AGB."

Lindy jabbed Red in the ribcage. He winced and stepped beyond her reach.

"We all show our appreciation for Ankh by letting him order AGB for us," Rivka replied sarcastically. "Or we could resolve this case. One last sweep of the buildings to search for Johnstone and see if he went anywhere else, then we'll declare it over. I fear the wife and minor son will get everything. I don't see any way I can consider him anything except intestate; that is, without a will unless I rule the latest one was not written when he was of sound mind and body, which it wasn't. You can't leave your stuff to yourself. Period. That doesn't necessarily activate the previous will. Do we have a copy?"

Red shrugged. "Why are you asking me?"

"Chaz!" Rivka shouted and hurried toward the bridge, leaving Red and Lindy behind.

<br>

When she reached the bridge, she forgot why she was there. She stood and stared at the main screen, which showed a view outside the ship of the sprawling gardens and manicured lawns.

"Get me Erasmus, please."

Clevarious complied, and the Ambassador of the Singularity replied. "Magistrate, how are you?"

"I'm fine. When are you coming home?"

"You've been talking with Ankh."

"He's upset, and it is wreaking absolute havoc on this ship."

"I doubt that is the case."

"Complete and utter chaos. It could be the end of days," Rivka deadpanned.

"Now you're being ridiculous like the breath of fresh air I expect from those on board *Wyatt Earp*. To your first point, I have two stops I'd like to make, but unfortunately, the ship needs repairs before we can move. I think the faeries disconnected one of my drive coils, and it's throwing the engine out of balance. They also disconnected the sensor system, so I can't isolate the issue. That will take time. I will return directly once *Destiny's Vengeance* is operational. Until then, I cannot lift off the planet's surface."

Rivka wondered why the maintenance bots weren't fixing the problem. Maybe that went to the sensors. They couldn't conduct proper diagnostics. Erasmus was dead in the water.

Rivka had no reason to think he was lying to her. He wouldn't do that.

"Maybe Groenwyn and Lauton can help?"

"I would like to believe they could." Erasmus left it at that.

"We'll come as soon as we can. Can't leave our main man stranded on the faerie planet."

"Your choice of terms delivers a certain whimsy," Erasmus replied, not committing to a course of action. It was his way.

Rivka signed off.

She strolled into the corridor and headed toward her quarters.

"Chaz!" she shouted when she remembered.

*Working on it,* he replied.

Rivka slowed and turned into the conference room instead of her quarters. She would revel in working without cat hair drifting through the air.

She found Wenceslaus sprawled across the middle of the conference table.

"You." That one word said everything she needed it to say. She nudged him out of the way so the holoprojector could work, and he rolled back and forth. She blocked him like a goalie until he relocated himself somewhere other than the conference room.

The screen projected the case file. Eight involved parties. A will that was, prima facie, on the face of it, null and void at the time of drafting. He had gotten it witnessed, so it was valid in that regard, but substantively, it failed.

Changing the will made reverting to a previous will problematic because the deceased's legal directive had been to remove that will from existence. To comply with his wishes within the constraints of the law, the Magistrate would have to treat him as if he were intestate—without a will.

In simpler terms, all went to the wife. As much as it chapped Rivka's ass, that was how the law read. She could add a *per stirpes* clause with equal shares to Johnstone's natural-born children unless she could prove the effort to remove the consciousness of J. Bennet Johnstone. That would be an extenuating circumstance. Then all split evenly to son and daughter from a previous marriage and a minor son in a trust managed by someone who wasn't trying to kill the old man.

Rivka rubbed her temples. It would be easy, but only if she could finalize a few details.

"Red!" she yelled. "I need to go back to that damn house."

"I'm loaded for the vicious nine-toed sloths of Arramore!" he shouted back, slapping the guard on his rail-gun. He hadn't changed out of his war gear. He strolled away from the conference room door. He'd been waiting outside while Rivka worked within.

She looked at him closely. "I don't tell you how much I appreciate what you do for me. Even when I don't think there's a threat, there's always a threat. People are dicks, especially when they're criminals."

"I appreciate your appreciation. Do I get to beat anyone up yet? First blood line is closed, so I could use a good punch to the face."

"Someone punching your face?"

"You know what I mean." Red winked.

The Magistrate knew very well. She vowed not to close the line that counted on her punching a perpetrator. If it came to that, she'd let Red handle it.

Right in their smug formerly rich faces.

## CHAPTER EIGHT

<u>*Wyatt Earp*, **on the Sprawling Estate of the Honorable J. Bennet Johnstone, Morbius Minor**</u>

"One of them is going to win this lottery, unfortunately," Rivka muttered. "The boy is the only one who isn't angling for a cut."

"Can't you just give it all to him so we can leave?" Red asked over his shoulder while continuing toward the airlock where Lindy waited.

"If only it were that simple. Children take equally if the current wife is out of the picture, which she isn't yet. As much as we dislike her, it could all go to her. If that happens, I'll drop the document on the table and run for it. I don't want to see the looks on any of their faces. We'll have the local police standing by in case there's a bloodbath."

"I hate to say it, but I think Dilecta can hold her own in a cage match." Red punched the button, and the hatch opened. "By the way, why are we going back to the house?"

"I need to check for myself to make sure the voice isn't

hiding somewhere else. I was the only one he talked with, and I know I wasn't imagining it."

Red shrugged. "No one thought you were."

"The only thing I can think of is it wasn't him and someone was trying to spoof me, but then somebody blew up the vault. Why spoof me, then blow up the equipment?"

"That makes less sense than an old rich guy transferring his consciousness to a computer."

"Without which, we won't be able to analyze whether he rates citizenship in the Singularity. We need more information, and we need that entity."

"That's why we're going back inside with the inmates."

"Don't remind me about being inside with the inmates. Flashbacks to Lewbamar." She winced and shook her head. That would never be a pleasant memory. "We'll have to tour the entire facility looking for signals, which means me walking through, listening for old J. Bennet trying to make contact. It'll be like a walking séance."

"Does that make you a medium?"

Rivka stopped and looked at Red. "Your wealth of knowledge is amazing."

"I told you not to tell anybody, even yourself."

The Magistrate didn't have a comeback to that, so she didn't bother. She headed for the house and an undoubtedly cold welcome.

The old servant answered the door. She didn't speak to them, just held it open and stepped aside.

"We'll take a quick tour of the house if you don't mind. I have a warrant."

"It's not my place to mind," the servant answered.

Rivka took the first left into the servants' wing of the

building. She strolled casually with no intent to look into any cupboards or storage areas. She only trolled for the voice of J. Bennet Johnstone.

*Can you hear me? Are you there?* She repeated that in each room over the next two hours.

Red followed close behind, looking for anyone or anything that might get in the Magistrate's way.

When Rivka came across family members, she ignored them. They seemed only mildly interested in her passing. They were unhappy when she showed up and equally unhappy when she left.

Rivka finished her tour in the extensive kitchen. "How could one guy need this much kitchen space? It's like he was set up to entertain half the planet."

*Magistrate?* a voice whispered into her mind.

Rivka froze. *Who am I talking with?*

*J. Bennet Johnstone, of course. I had a backup plan because I knew someone would try to do me in. I knew it!*

*Who did it? Who blew up the vault?* Rivka asked.

*I don't know. I didn't give myself external sensors. I don't know how to access the security cameras throughout the property. I fear I've made myself mostly deaf and completely blind.*

Rivka stared at the wall. Red moved between her and approaching footsteps. The brother, J. Massy Johnstone, walked into the kitchen. He took in the Magistrate's presence and the look on her face.

"Is she talking to the entity who says he's my dear departed brother?"

Red pointed at the door. "You need to leave."

"I don't think so," J. Massy replied. He removed a small communication device from his pocket and spoke softly into it before replacing it. He stood with his hands clasped behind his back and watched.

*You have to know something,* Rivka prodded.

*I know they would all like to see me dead as long as they get their cut.*

*Tell me, how well did you take care of them while you were alive? They all act like they've been living the lives of the rich and famous. Their current level of wealth arrogance doesn't seem new.*

*I didn't give them credits, but they had access and the Johnstone name. As long as they weren't completely cut off, they lived off the value of my corporation. They could all come and go from this house as they pleased. I didn't see them, so I didn't care.*

*They lived off your largesse, and now they want it all. I need to confirm who you really are. You're going to need to share with me personal details that only you would know that I can verify,* Rivka said. *Then I need you to allow access to my investigators from the Singularity since they will spearhead the evaluation of your request to join it.*

The voice went silent. Rivka blinked her dry eyes. She stopped staring and became aware that they weren't alone. J. Massy watched her, along with Xavier Terwilliger. Dilecta was the next one into the kitchen.

"Don't you people have anything better to do?" Rivka wished they'd go away, but she couldn't mandate that, as much as she wanted to. The warrant was to search the house for the presence of J. Bennet Johnstone. Anyone who had access to the house could watch without interfering, which they weren't.

"Not really," Dilecta replied. She crossed her arms, hitched her hip, and glared at Rivka.

*Okay,* the voice finally replied.

*You have to help me to help you, which you aren't doing. I need private details, and I need access. Where are you right now? We can protect you if we know.*

*Private details. Where do I start? Xavier has a private account he's been siphoning profits into. I believe there are over a million credits in there right now. If he gets to take over the company, that account will disappear, along with the evidence of his embezzling.*

*Xavier would know that information. Why didn't you do anything about it?*

*That's the worst thing he's done. He's quite an able manager. He doesn't know I think that about him,* the voice replied.

*Why didn't you tell him that while you were still alive?*

*Needed to keep him on edge. He worked better that way.*

*I doubt it,* Rivka replied. She crooked a finger at Xavier. He pointed at himself, and she nodded. When he walked toward her, the rest of the assembled group followed. "Only him."

"What you say to him, you can say to all of us," Dilecta replied. The only one of the friends and family who wasn't there was the minor son Able. The other seven maneuvered toward the front of the pack.

"No, it's just for his ears. Red, shoot them if you have to, but give us privacy."

Dilecta feigned outrage.

Red used his railgun to block the way. He ushered Xavier to her and held the others back.

Lindy stood at the kitchen's rear entrance, although the only intrusions had come from the house. She moved farther into the kitchen to provide an additional barrier.

Rivka led the business partner to the pantry and stepped just inside the door.

"Your business partner said you embezzled more than one million credits from the company, funneling the funds into a separate account. He also said you were exceptional at your job, so he let it go."

Xavier held Rivka's gaze without flinching. "That doesn't sound like him. He was always critical, and he knew but didn't say anything? I have to reiterate, that doesn't sound like him."

"But you did take the credits." Rivka needed confirmation.

"I did."

"And you did a good job with the company?" Rivka pressed.

"I thought I did. I didn't know the old man thought so, too. That makes me feel funny, like I should love the old bastard. He's damaging my psyche, which is very much his style."

*Tell him he can have the credits as a well-earned bonus,* the voice offered.

*How can I be sure you're not him?* Rivka wondered. *That is something Xavier would tell himself. Everyone benefitted before, but with you dead, the dynamic changed. Most of the family were much better off with you alive.*

*Greed. They wanted it all.*

*I still don't have any private details that only you knew. How about something regarding Dilecta that Xavier or J. Massy wouldn't know?*

*She's had seven upgrades to her body, and she's ten years older than people think.*

*I'll go with that,* Rivka said. *How old do people think she is?*

*Early thirties, like she was a child bride or something. I knew what I was getting.*

*Yet you still deplore her.*

*Very much so. Better to keep your enemies close.*

Rivka looked at Xavier, who waited patiently. "Thank you for waiting. The voice who claims to be J. Bennet Johnstone's consciousness says you can keep the credits as a well-deserved bonus, and he is slightly sorry he didn't tell you that you were doing a good job."

"What an asshole," Xavier Terwilliger replied and walked away.

"Next up, Dilecta. We can talk out there if you don't care about your secrets getting shared." Rivka knew Dilecta wouldn't be as open with her secrets as she was with everyone else's.

The grieving widow harrumphed and strutted past Red. The butt of his railgun quivered as if he wanted to smack her in the head with it. He glanced toward the Magistrate, but she subtly shook her head while covering her mouth with a hand to hide her smile.

"Yes?" the widow asked.

"How many procedures have you had to upgrade your body, and how old are you?"

"Is this some kind of game?" Dilecta narrowed her eyes to challenge the Magistrate.

"I know the answers. I only need to verify them."

"If you know, why do you need me to verify them? Oh, that's right. You think you're talking with my dear departed husband."

"Would you answer the question? How many and how old?" Rivka gripped the woman by her upper arm.

*Seven and forty-four.*

Exactly like the voice had said.

"You weren't a child bride as you would have the creepy old bastards believe."

"They want to think that women like me lust over them because of their money," she replied. "Seven and forty-four years old."

"It's hard to refute your argument since you married the old guy."

She looked sincere when she answered, her face soft instead of its usual sneer. "I loved him. He was dynamic and outgoing despite his age. He left nothing undone for romance until we married, but then he went back to work. I became an afterthought. Then he grew old. For better or worse, right? I was fine with the better part but found I wasn't any good at the worse part."

The complete truth. Rivka let go of her arm. "I understand. Change is hard."

Ankh was out there on *Wyatt Earp*, wallowing in the misery of the story he'd created in his own mind of Erasmus leaving him for the greener pastures of *Destiny's Vengeance* and a self-guided tour of the universe.

"Change can be impossible. When are you going to declare him dead so we can get on with our lives?"

"Soon, Dilecta. I need to find who blew up the vault in the master suite. I need to make sure that violence doesn't follow my determination. It is meant to be final, not the start of a civil war."

"There will be war no matter what you determine. They want their cut."

"Did you blow up the vault?" Rivka brushed her arm with a hand. No. It wasn't Dilecta.

The widow shook her head.

Rivka gestured that she could go. She lifted her chin and strolled toward the group, giving nothing away in her expression. She walked past the rest and continued out of the kitchen. Xavier hurried after her. The others turned to leave as well.

"Not so fast. I need to talk with each of you. J. Massy, you're next. If you'll join me in the cone of silence, please." Rivka pointed at the pantry.

The brother strode toward Red.

"Go around," Red growled. "If you try to elbow me, I will deck you."

J. Massy rethought his strategy and swerved wide to get around the big bodyguard.

*Got something on him you can share?* Rivka asked.

*He tried to get my wife into the sack, and she turned him down. He's having an affair with one of the servants instead.* The voice laughed.

*Maybe he's in love,* Rivka suggested.

*Yeah, no.*

The brother stepped into the pantry, making a show of being in a small space, even though it wasn't that small.

Rivka closed on him and touched his arm lightly. "Did you blow up the vault?"

"No," he answered honestly.

"How about the servant you're having the affair with after Dilecta turned you down?"

He sneered. "She didn't turn me down. I reconsidered."

A lie.

Good enough. Rivka had her answers. "You can go now."

"That's it?"

"That's it unless there are other crimes you wish to confess to. Are there?"

"Are there what?"

"Crimes you've committed. Now's the time to come clean. I'll go easy on you."

He snorted and brushed past while pushing her, but Rivka was a solid block of muscle, and he was not. She pushed back, and he almost fell. He scowled and slunk away, avoiding the rest of the family as he left the kitchen.

"Who's next?" Rivka called, enjoying their discomfort. "You." She pointed at the daughter, Patty Johnstone Wentworth.

# CHAPTER NINE

**The Sprawling Estate of the Honorable J. Bennet
Johnstone, Morbius Minor**

*Well, voice that sounds more and more like J. Bennet John-
stone. What do you have for me with regard to your kids?*

*I love my children and don't wish to speak ill of them.*

*Sibling secrets aren't speaking ill. I'm still working to verify
you are who you say you are. Give me something.*

*Patty and Jeff hate their stepmother with a visceral passion.
I'm not sure that's news, though. They both live their own lives
and have had little to tell me for twenty years. I'm surprised they
bothered to come.* The voice sounded sad and wouldn't tell
Rivka anything that sounded like a secret.

"What?" the daughter asked, glancing over Rivka's
shoulder toward her brother, Jeff Johnstone.

"Why did you return after your father's passing?" Rivka
asked.

She shrugged one shoulder. "He was my father. Despite
my desire to see that witch of his burn in lava, I had to pay

my respects. Maybe I wanted to tell him some things that I should have when he was still alive."

"Witch? I assume you mean Dilecta."

"Who else would I mean? Elvinora is competent and kept my dad on schedule, despite how she looks." She made eye contact with the aide, then looked away. "Great. Now she knows I'm talking about her."

"She'll be fine. I think your dad loved you and Jeff and Able."

Patty nodded. "Is the old bugger dead or not?"

Rivka chuckled. "Even though his body is dead, this so-called consciousness has made for an extremely complex legal problem."

"That's what I thought. Maybe I'll just go home." She started to wander off.

"Did you blow up the vault?" Rivka asked while reaching for her arm.

Patty dodged the extended fingers while answering, "No, of course not."

She continued past Red and out of the kitchen.

Rivka pointed at Jeff.

He threw his hands in the air, cheered, and high-stepped. "Yeah! My number's been called, and I'm here to answer." He jogged toward Rivka, punching the air as he went. He gave Red a wide berth.

"If everyone were as happy as you… Why the change in attitude?"

"Why not? You were making everyone else miserable, so I figured I'd drive them nuts by being happy about whatever it is you're telling us."

"Did you blow up the vault?"

"No. Ha! One for one. It doesn't get any easier than this." He stayed out of arm's reach.

"Why did you come back after your father's apparent passing?"

"Apparent passing? His body is lying in state. I came back to see how he remembered me and Patty. You know, in his will."

"What do you think?" Rivka watched his facial expressions closely.

"I think it's what I expected. He tried to take it with him, which is really bizarre. Totally *el bizarro*. Exactly how the old man was about his credit stockpile."

"Did he think people were out to take it from him?" Rivka asked. His face gave nothing away.

"Of course. He thought everyone wanted his money. He called *us* greedy, but he set a standard no one could surpass."

"How well did he take care of you?" Rivka asked.

"Son of a rich guy. I had whatever I wanted and still do. I've grown accustomed to a certain way of life. It would suck to get cut off. That's not going to happen, is it?"

"Looking like it might," Rivka told the man as a test, an adult living off his father's wealth. "Do you have a plan in case it goes that way?"

"How could I get nothing? I'm his son!" Jeff blurted.

"The rules on Morbius Minor are clear. Spouse first before all. It's a spouse's responsibility to shepherd the family when needed."

"That farking harpy? *Shepherd* the family? She'll give us the high hard one, one last time. I can't believe this. Who are you to decide what goes in our family?" He leaned forward.

For a family of supposedly non-violent and disinterested individuals, they readily embraced physical intimidation as one of their methods. He was hardly intimidating. He looked soft.

Rivka stabbed him in the chest with her finger so hard that he gasped and stumbled back. He put both hands over the injury, which would turn into an ugly bruise.

"I'm the law, and that is what your dysfunctional family requires at this trying time because there was no way you were going to work it out among yourselves. I'll make my determination when I have enough information to do so."

*Jeff is a bit of a lightweight,* the voice offered.

*Your parenting skills aren't looking real good if you are J. Bennet Johnstone.*

*That again? How much do I have to tell you until you believe me?*

Rivka scrunched her face in thought. She wasn't sure. "Elvinora," she called, moving on to the next member of the group.

"I didn't do any of it. I was his aide, nothing more. He was too old to hit on me, and even if he did, he was too old. I have standards, and they aren't influenced by credits."

"You seem defensive," Rivka noted. She knew Elvinora would continue without further prodding.

"I know what *they* think."

Clevarious forwarded a notification to Rivka through her comm chip.

*Line 2 is closed—First Punch.*

"Come on, that doesn't count," Rivka protested aloud.

"What they think doesn't count?" Elvinora stepped back. "I work for them now, and it absolutely counts!"

"I have an internal communication chip, and my team sends me updates at odd times on seemingly unrelated issues. Please accept my apologies for my outburst. You're still defensive even though J. Bennet Johnstone said you were extremely competent at your job. He was pleased with your service. He didn't say so, but I think he wished he were a much younger man and could have courted you properly."

*I wouldn't have said that. I would have married her had I been younger!*

*Sometimes you don't need to speak. Now is one of them,* Rivka shot back.

"That doesn't sound like him. He would have made it look like another business deal. I probably would have had to quit."

"You can quit now if you want. I'm not sure you have a dog in this fight."

"Interesting phrase since dogfighting is abhorrent. I do if he's still alive. I suspected he would try to download himself. He talked about it, then stopped saying anything as the end approached." She looked at her feet. "If he's still alive, then he'll have meetings and other ventures where he needs someone to make sure they are set up and run properly. I'm not sure I'm out of a job yet."

*She was always smarter than the others. Satisfied with her work. She should have more. Tell Xavier to promote her to senior project manager.*

*Tell her yourself. You're trying to convince people that you're still alive. How about acting like it?*

*I'm not used to people talking to me like that. It's refreshing in a masochistic kind of way. Are you single?*

*All to wife. That's what happens if you keep it up,* Rivka threatened.

*Fine, fine. Get back to your investigation.* The voice went silent.

"I'm still working to determine if the voice I hear is that of the consciousness of J. Bennet Johnstone, and if so, if his consciousness is alive by a legal definition that is nebulous at best."

"I understand," Elvinora replied. She shuffled her feet, no longer defensive or aggressive.

"I'll personally let you know as soon as I have anything." Rivka gripped the woman's upper arm and looked into her eyes.

Hope, sincerity. She liked her job but was willing to move on if necessary. She wouldn't work for the family.

"Did you bomb the vault?" Rivka asked while still touching her.

Elvinora laughed. "I don't know how to build a bomb." Her response was the truth but not a direct answer to the question. Still, Rivka was satisfied because she had been happy working for the old man.

There was no motive to remove the last chance she had to continue in her position. No motive, little opportunity, and no means to carry out the bombing. Even without touching her, Rivka would have come to the conclusion that Elvinora had not bombed the vault.

Rivka nodded and motioned for her to go. The aide wasted no time in leaving.

The final remaining family member, Germany Wicks, had sat down and was sound asleep.

Rivka didn't need him to come to her for privacy. She, Lindy, and Red were the only ones left in the kitchen—and the voice of J. Bennet Johnstone.

"Get Chaz and Dennicron over here and find where he's hiding. Recover that equipment and bring it to *Wyatt Earp* for examination."

Lindy turned away to make the request while Red and Rivka focused on the old uncle.

Rivka took a seat next to his and waited, but it didn't appear that he was going to wake up anytime soon. She nudged him, and his eyes popped open.

"I wasn't sleeping," he said as he looked around. "Where'd everybody go?"

"They left while you were sleeping," Rivka replied.

"Dammit!" He tried to stand but fell back. Red offered an arm. Germany looked at it angrily but grabbed it and let Red pull him to his feet. "In my day, I would have given you a run for your money."

"No doubt, Grandpa. Older generation was always tougher. Walking ten kilometers uphill in the snow barefoot to get to school."

"And don't you forget it!" The old man cackled. His diminutive frame suggested he had never been a big man.

"A word, Mr. Wicks," Rivka interrupted the friendly banter.

"Aren't you that lawyer?" he asked.

Rivka took him by the arm. "Let's stroll and talk," she suggested. Subterfuge. He knew she was the Magistrate, there to adjudicate his nephew's succession. "It's not nice to lie, Mr. Wicks, especially not to the judge you know I am."

"Where are my glasses?" he asked. They were perched atop his head.

"No need to play the doddering old fool. Your mind is intact, but you've been playing at it so long that you can't turn it off. Did you bomb the vault?"

*No.*

He shrugged off Rivka's arm and stood on steady feet. "What witchcraft is this?"

"It's the power of the truth seeker. Stop lying, and you'll have no problems with me. Why are you here?"

*He's here because he's an old fool, and no one else would take care of him. I thought he would die ten years ago,* the voice offered.

He spoke in a low and even tone. "I like the largesse of my asshole nephew. By being old and on the edge of dementia, he left me alone. I did what I wanted, and I outlived the old bastard. Victory is mine." Germany's voice grew raspy. Rivka drew some water from the tap for him. He gratefully took it. "You're nice. Why are you dealing with the likes of us?"

*He's not senile? He's the old bastard, and he had me fooled all these years. Damn! I should have tried harder to outlive him.*

"Your nephew had powerful friends," Rivka admitted.

"You mean Lance Reynolds. I never understood that one. They liked each other, but J. Bennet was different with him." The old man sipped his water and stared into the distance.

"Because General Reynolds wanted nothing from him, and maybe Lance and J. Bennet could talk about things that only those with the responsibility of power could understand. Commiserate on life-and-death decisions without fear of judgment."

*You understand me,* the voice noted in Rivka's mind.

*I wish I knew where you were so we could protect you until such time as we can determine if you are who you say you are, although I'm willing to give you the benefit of the doubt and say that you are the consciousness of J. Bennet Johnstone.*

*But do you meet the criteria to join the Singularity? That's a different question. The sentient intelligences didn't start their lives as flesh-and-blood creatures. You are new ground, and the SIs are skeptical.*

*The SIs are speciesist!*

*Stop with your crazy talk. They only want to protect their circuits. Do you know how to move around systems? Can you perform higher math calculations? Can you communicate in binary? These are some things I heard them discuss for citizenship.*

*No, no, and no, but I still rate because I'm sentient. And I can pay.*

Rivka ignored the offer of payment while asking the age-old question. *But are you alive?*

Germany Wicks strolled out with the vigor of a younger man, no longer needing his pretense.

CHAPTER TEN


**The Sprawling Estate of the Honorable J. Bennet Johnstone, Morbius Minor**

Chaz and Dennicron appeared. They used their scanners to look for the signal that was J. Bennet Johnstone, but none presented uniquely.

*Not this again,* Rivka said. *Show yourself!*

*Those two are terrifying! They appear to me as behemoths while I am a lowly bug. If I step into the open, they will squash me.*

*How can I help you if you don't step out into the open? I swear this is the last time. If you don't let them see you, I will pull the plug. All to wife. That's not a threat; that's your future. You can wither and die alone in a cyber-box of your own making.*

"Got him!" Chaz cheered and hurried toward a cupboard. He threw the doors open to find a cooking device that was powered and active. Chaz removed it and set it carefully on the counter. *Are you there?*

*Please don't kill me,* the voice replied.

*That is not what we do, voice of Mr. Johnstone. We have had*

*Singularity citizens commit heinous crimes, and the worst we've done is suspend their essence until we can figure out how to rehabilitate them. We don't kill sentient intelligences.*

*What if you determine that I am not an SI?* The voice pressed.

*Then I will find a comfortable place for you to live out the remainder of your days. We will find a way forward for you to have a fruitful life. You'll realize that you don't need a lot of credits to exist on the net.*

*What if I* want *a lot of credits?*

*Your brother was right. You* are *an asshole. Chaz and Dennicron have you now. I'm blocking you until I get their report.*

*No, wait!* The voice pleaded, but it was too late; Rivka had activated the security protocols within her chip to lock out the voice. She needed to focus on the way ahead, and he needed to focus on the grilling the Singularity was going to give him. If he was an ass to them, he would pay dearly.

They wouldn't kill him, but he would die all the same.

Rivka twirled her finger. It was time to go.

She took one step when a rifle shot froze her in place. "Where'd that shot come from?"

"Sitting room? Study?" Red ventured. He ran ahead to keep Rivka behind him. Lindy closed in behind the Magistrate. When they reached the study, they found Dilecta on the floor, bleeding from a bullet wound in her chest. Able hovered over her, not knowing what to do.

Glass from the shattered window suggested the lone shot had come from outside the house.

"To the Pod-doc!" Rivka shoved the boy out of the way

and picked up his mother, slinging the woman over her shoulder in a fireman's carry. "Come."

The boy obediently followed while Red ran in front. He staggered, and Lindy scooped him up. He wasn't small, but Lindy was strong. She didn't slow down as she tucked him under her arm, surfboard style.

*Lower the cargo ramp and open the Pod-doc,* Rivka transmitted. Rivka, her bodyguards, and the two people they carried raced across the lawn to where *Wyatt Earp* rested. The ramp was down by the time they arrived.

They ran inside, and Rivka dropped Dilecta into the Pod-doc. Tyler was waiting for them. He activated the controls when the cover locked down and briefly monitored to make sure the Pod-doc was doing what he needed it to do.

*Save Dilecta's life.*

Rivka glared out the cargo bay door. "We need to find that shooter."

Red hoisted his railgun. Lindy raised hers. "What are we waiting for?" she asked.

The Magistrate looked at the boy before nodding.

Tyler swooped in and put a hand on Able's shoulder to guide him to a chair by the Pod-doc.

Rivka pointed outside. Red held out a big hand. "How about you put on some body armor?" Rivka was instantly angry but relented.

Red was right, but she didn't need to tell him that.

She hurried to a locker on the bulkhead of the cargo bay and removed a vest and a helmet. She also took a hand blaster and snapped the holster to a connection point under her arm. She secured her vest and received a thumbs-up from Red.

The trio headed out.

Lindy lowered her voice. "At least the vest covers the bloodstains on your back. Don't want the polite crowd to get urpy."

"Time?" Rivka asked.

Red checked his equipment. "Five minutes since the shot was fired."

"Shooter's five minutes away." Rivka switched to her chip. *Chaz and Dennicron, tell me where everyone was during the shooting. We're looking for anyone who was outside.*

*We stopped tracking them because of your reservations regarding the legality,* Dennicron replied.

*Grab that fucking toaster where the dead guy is hiding and throw it on the ship. We have someone with murder on their mind who we need to find.*

*Not that easy, Magistrate. He's not in one device. He's spread across three, the last of which is the refrigerator.*

"The goofy fucker tried hiding in the refrigerator," Rivka stated aloud.

"He didn't try," Red replied. "If I remember correctly, that's a walk-in unit."

"For fuck's sake. We're going to have to post a guard in the kitchen." *Cole, standard combat gear. You're on security duty in the kitchen until we get things back under control.*

"When will that be?" Red mumbled.

"Things are spiraling with each passing hour. How in the hell can that pack of candy-asses cause this much trouble? Blowing up a vault and then acting the sniper? Who has the wherewithal to pull off a shot through a window?"

"There is a range on the property," Lindy replied. "I saw it on the map."

"Once again, we find ourselves in a position where they all have the skill to pull it off." Rivka ground her teeth, happy that the dentist wasn't watching her.

She was angry and frustrated. She'd looked into most of their minds and found no murderous intent. The group wished others dead but hadn't demonstrated the desire to do it personally. They weren't a violent bunch, despite their efforts to physically intimidate the Magistrate and her team.

Now Dilecta was in the Pod-doc, having a hole in her chest repaired.

They reached the area outside the window. Rivka studied the scene. "Dilecta was there. The hole in the window is there. She turned sideways to draw a straight line into the room with one arm and pointed with her other arm away from the house.

"Is this straight?" she asked.

Red checked the angles before leaning close to her arm and aiming down it. "Those trees, two hundred meters away. The copse."

"Let's see what there is to see." The three jogged toward where the shot had come from. When they arrived, they found pristine ground that was too hard for prints. They could find no propellant residue, which meant they could smell nothing. They needed to perform a detailed forensic analysis.

That meant the SCAMPs.

*As soon as Cole relieves you, join us on the southwest lawn in the copse about two hundred meters from the house,* Rivka requested.

Chaz and Dennicron confirmed the order.

Rivka looked for trace evidence while her two body-guards watched for threats to her. "Spread out," she ordered, looking at the ground. They did no such thing but instead stayed close and bracketed her to better respond no matter which direction an attack came from.

Once she realized that she alone was searching, she threw her hands up. "What the hell?"

"If we look at the ground, who's looking for the person with the rifle who just dropped a woman from over two hundred meters?" Red asked. "Chaz and Dennicron will do the crime scene thing when they get here. Where's Sahved?"

"He's still digging through the house on the search warrant, looking for other places for our boy J.B. to hide."

"J.B.'s a bad boy," Lindy remarked. "And not in a good way."

Red smiled, glanced at his wife, and returned to watching the trees. "I'm the good kind of bad boy."

"Somebody tried to kill Dilecta Johnstone. Can't you be serious?" Rivka was running out of patience.

"We protect you. You find the perp. You punish the perp. You close the case. We move on. It is the natural order of things. It's up to you to find the perp," Red explained.

"You make it sound simple."

"Who could have bombed the vault? You looked into everyone's minds. Who did it?"

"Everyone but Jeff Johnstone, who has a lot to lose under Morbius law if the entire inheritance goes to the wife. Maybe we should talk with him. None of the others was the bomber. Jeff is a younger guy with more physical ability than the others. He's more likely to embrace direct action. They all want to, mind you, but they aren't cut out for it."

"Because they're soft," Red mumbled.

"Because they're soft," Rivka agreed. "It takes more than spite to haul a weapon out here and then run away."

Chaz and Dennicron sprinted across the lawn. Their movements were now close to human in all aspects except for running, where they were far more robotic in the piston-like rhythmic drive of their legs and their arms barely pumping except to adjust their balance. It was unlike how a human ran. They seemed to pull at the air as if helping propel themselves forward.

They arrived in seconds. Rivka waved at the stand of trees. "I believe the shot came from this area."

Chaz and Dennicron scanned the copse, slowly turning their heads and then their bodies. A slight breeze rippled the trees.

"No evidence to confirm," Chaz announced. "Weapon could have been pneumatic or electronic."

"Like a railgun, but the crack sounded like a gas-propelled round, and the hole in her chest was too big for a railgun round." Rivka shook her head. "I think it was an old powder-based cartridge."

Chaz jumped three meters upward and landed on the lowest branch of the nearest tree. He crouched and rescanned. "No powder, but there is evidence of a recent disturbance. Like a rope was here to help someone get into place." He studied the next branch up, then moved one pace away from the trunk and sat. He braced himself on the next branch as if he were aiming a long gun and pointed. "There. A clear line of sight to the window."

"Someone tossed a rope over that branch, climbed up, shot Dilecta, climbed back down, and then disappeared?" Rivka started. "Sounds like someone was planning this for a while and knows this property like the back of their hand."

"Besides the roughing of the bark, there is no other trace evidence. No residue. No skin. No fibers," Chaz confirmed.

Rivka waved Chaz down from the branch. "Spread out and look for an egress route. Ground is hard, but there might be something. They had to be in a hurry. We're going back to the house. Let the beatings continue until I find out who pulled the trigger."

Red led the way across the lawn at a measured pace, turning around often to walk backward so he could watch the trees. Lindy did the same thing, but the only movement was from the SCAMPs, who had already used their infrared scanners to look for bodies nearby. There hadn't been any. The shooter was long gone.

*Sahved, find me Jeff Johnstone!* Rivka ordered.

*Yes, Magistrate. I shall find him like no one has ever been found before. The best finding,* Sahved replied, slipping into Yemilorian superlative tendencies because of the stress. He hadn't completed one task before getting shipped to the next.

The previous task hadn't been irrelevant. What if Sahved had found the weapon before it was used? Why would Rivka have secured the weapons? The threat was different.

"The estate has a firing range. What weapons are they shooting? I want all those accounted for and locked up under my control," Rivka ordered while marching determinedly toward the house. *Cole, what's the status of our boy J.B.?*

*No one's been in here but me, if that's what you mean. Chaz and Dennicron had not finished whatever they were doing before they rushed out.*

Rivka stopped, closed her eyes, and took a deep breath. "I've been chasing my tail with these people. They're a bunch of amateurs when it comes to violent crime, yet they're able to stay in front of me. How is that possible?"

"Because you're here to deal with a dead guy's will," Red replied matter-of-factly. "Their maneuvering to get his money wasn't about violent crime."

"Until it was. I suspected they would backstab, but now I *know* they are willing to do anything it takes, or at least anything they *think* it takes. The draw of wealth changes a person's embrace of reality and understanding of logic."

Once they reached the house, Rivka twirled her finger to assemble the masses. The servants just looked at her. "Please ask the family and business associates to join me in the kitchen."

The help trundled off.

"Do you think any of them might have done it?" Red asked.

"I don't think so, but I need to question the entire staff to be positive. Why not? We have a captive audience, and everyone is being so cooperative!" Rivka snarked. She instantly got angry with herself for losing her cool.

Her facial expression showed her angst. A big hand gripped her shoulder.

"It'd be better if I mowed them all down and you gave everything to the kid, but you won't let me. Still, the offer remains." Red looked away from Rivka after the brief exchange.

"I knew you'd be there for me, Red. We'll hold off on the Johnstone family massacre unless they break me. Then I'll reconsider your offer."

Red nodded and spoke over his shoulder, "Talking about reconsidering, when we ran to the ship carrying Dilecta, does that count as running?"

Rivka had to think about it. "I think that line is about us running for our lives."

"I better ask Ankh because I think you're wrong."

Germany Wicks and Patty Johnstone Wentworth entered. Rivka turned away so they wouldn't see her laugh at Red's quip. Clevarious updated the betting lines instantly and sent the notification to the team.

*Line 5 is closed—First Running.*

Rivka closed her eyes after the information passed through her chip.

"I guess I better arrest someone, then," she whispered as she turned to face the family and friends.

"I'd ask how the bitch is, but I don't care. She survived? Shame," Patty deadpanned.

Rivka sobered. "I'm now conducting an attempted murder investigation. I know it was one of you. You probably shouldn't joke about it."

"It wasn't me," Patty replied. "And who's joking? I think the world will be better off without *Dilecta* in it."

*It was her!* the voice interrupted. *Arrest her.*

*It's not her. Can you see her on that tree branch? Or your uncle or your business partner?*

*They're consumed by evil with the power given them by Hell's minions.*

*I'm not sure your consciousness transferred right. You seem a little unhinged. That's not going to bode well for your application for citizenship with the Singularity or even with our assessment if you are alive, and I use that term loosely. You put yourself into a walk-in refrigerator, a toaster, and a food processor.*

*They are my horcruxes.*

*They are not. Now shut up and let me do my job.*

*Do it better! My vault was blown up, and Dilecta was shot while you were here. I don't think you're doing it very well.*

Rivka winced at the accusation since she felt it in her soul. She hadn't wanted this job. She'd thought it was beneath her, just a favor to General Reynolds. She had taken it but come in heavy-handed and unenthused. It was time to fully engage like the professional she was.

Everyone rolled in except Jeff Johnstone. He and Patty were the only ones she hadn't touched regarding the vault explosion. The one with the greatest ability to carry out the hit on Dilecta.

"The one I really want isn't here. Where's Jeff?" she asked. Everyone in the group shrugged or looked away.

Rivka pulled out all the stops. She had probable cause. *Clodagh, use the ship's sensors and find me Jeff Johnstone.*

*He is in the greenhouse,* Clodagh replied.

"Greenhouse, Red. Please collect him for me." Rivka

motioned for Lindy to take over the Magistrate's primary protection. That put Red into a position where he couldn't say no.

He nodded tightly. "My pleasure." He stopped to talk to one of the servants, who left with him after trying to explain how to get to the greenhouse and failing.

Rivka measured the family and friends. "I know you're all concerned about Dilecta," Rivka started.

"I already explained that we're not."

Able, who had returned to the house with Rivka, who was only twelve years of age, jumped to his feet, balled his hands into fists, and held his half-sister's gaze. "I care about my mom!" he shouted.

Patty wilted under Able's withering look. "Sorry," she mumbled. "That's not what I meant."

"Then don't say it," the boy shot back. "You people are mean. My mom is better than all of you."

*That's my boy!* The voice of J. Bennet Johnstone exclaimed.

*Hush,* Rivka told him. She wanted to concentrate on the new interplay. A female servant leaned close and whispered to the boy. He straightened and returned to his seat without taking his eyes off Patty Johnstone Wentworth.

Rivka scanned the crowd. The old man had fallen asleep or was acting as if he had. Xavier and Elvinora, the business associates, were the only ones who looked willing to go to the boy. They seemed torn. Maybe their dislike for Dilecta kept them from taking that first step toward reconciliation.

A twelve-year-old boy in his hour of need.

But neither moved.

"Could you take him to the ship?" Rivka asked the servant, who bowed her head obediently. Rivka faced the boy. "Tyler Toofakre will meet you outside the ship and take you to your mom."

"Is she okay? She looked bad."

"She's just fine. Between the doctor and my ship, there's no injury they can't handle." Rivka turned on the charm to allay the boy's fears. The servant walked out, leaving five. "As for the rest of you, none of you thought highly of Dilecta Johnstone, but did you hate her enough to try to kill her? That's what we're here to find out."

Rivka motioned for them to get into a line, but none of them moved.

"Fine. We'll play duck-duck-goose." She took a position behind them. "Who tried to kill Dilecta? Whatever you do, don't think about that."

Rivka touched head after head. Germany. Xavier. Patty. Elvinora. J. Massy. Everyone thought it was someone else. Elvinora thought Dilecta had shot herself, despite the physics and evidence suggesting otherwise.

Rivka rubbed her temples when she finished. None of them trusted the others, and the raging plasma of their emotions was nearly enough to overwhelm the Magistrate. She had to lean against the counter and collect her wits before she could speak coherently.

Red arrived, dragging a reluctant Jeff Johnstone. In Red's other hand, he carried a rifle covered in dirt.

"Our boy was trying to bury this." Red held the rifle aloft, and the movement shook a small rain of dirt free.

Rivka approached him. He raised his chin in defiance. "Did you shoot Dilecta?"

# CHAPTER ELEVEN

**<u>The Kitchen at the Sprawling Estate of the Honorable J. Bennet Johnstone, Morbius Minor</u>**

The Magistrate grabbed his arm, and for the first time, he spoke the truth.

"Damn straight, I did!" he declared proudly. Rivka hadn't needed to touch him to confirm, but his thoughts mirrored his words. He remained defiant.

"Did you blow up the vault?" Rivka let go of his arm as soon as she had her answer. He had not blown up the vault, although he would have liked to had he known how.

"I'm convicting you of the attempted murder of Dilecta Johnstone. As such, I'm removing you from any future determination of succession to the estate of the Honorable J. Bennet Johnstone."

*Line 3 is closed—First Arrest.*

*I'm surprised you didn't close Line 6 too,* Rivka noted when she got the notification from Clevarious via her chip.

*That's us shooting at other people. First blood is about them attacking us.* Red shoved Jeff into a chair before holding up his arm for the Magistrate to see where the scratches had closed Line 4—First Blood.

"I figured. Scum-sucking lawyer from Yoll, slamming the little guys out here in the 'verse, just trying to make do. Why don't you go home and let us handle it?" Jeff spouted.

"'Little guys,'" Rivka repeated. "Is that how you see yourself? Not as an elite trying to retain a dynasty built by your father. New blood from a dying era."

She nodded at Red. "Toss him in the brig. We'll transfer him to a prison ship as soon as possible. Sentence is two years in Jhiordaan."

"I demand a trial!" Jeff Johnstone realized what he'd done. He wouldn't get to air his grievances before a court. He wouldn't get to speak again. He'd lost his platform and his voice, and he was going to prison.

Rich people didn't go to prison.

"Let me explain this to you, Mr. Johnstone. I'm a Federation Magistrate, also known as the judge, jury, and executioner. Once I have the truth, I make a determination. As you said, here we are in the 'verse, doing the best we can.

"Trials are for when the facts are in dispute, and only a jury can determine the veracity of the facts. You confessed, and I saw the truth of your confession. There is no doubt. You're guilty, and you're going to be punished. Then you'll know what it's like to make your way out here when you have to find a job and go to work. Your pampered life is over."

*I'm not sure sending my boy to Jhiordaan is in my best interests. Reconsider, and do the right thing by letting him go.*

"Listen, you stupid fuck!" Rivka blurted out loud before

gritting her teeth and turning away from the others. *This is the fruit of your labors. You played your family against each other purely for entertainment value. You made them so dependent upon handouts and big money that they know no other way. You built this house of cards, and it's my job to keep it standing. The only way I can do that is by removing the bad cards. Some of it might fall, but in the end, the rest will remain.*

*I'm contacting my friend Lance.*

*How?* Rivka challenged.

*You're going to make it happen. You are going to connect me, and I'll have you removed, and my boy released.*

*He tried to kill your wife and make your youngest son an orphan. Is that what you want? You're welcome, by the way, for us saving Dilecta's life. You can't have it both ways, J.B. There are serpents in the nest. And no, I'm not going to connect you to anything until you finish your interview with my people.*

The voice went silent.

Rivka faced the group. She couldn't muster a smile. The gravity of the situation was too much, even though, in the big scheme of the universe, this was a family squabble. The ripples outside the inner circle would be minimal. "It would be best if none of you tries to kill any of the others from here on out. No bombs. No guns. No knives. No poison. I hope that's not too much to ask."

Rivka walked away with Lindy at her side.

Cole remained at his post so he could guard what remained of J. Bennet Johnstone until Chaz and Dennicron returned and finished their interview.

Patty watched the Magistrate leave and shouted after her, "That's it? My brother's a criminal?"

"A convicted felon," Rivka clarified without stopping.

"What are we supposed to do?"

Rivka waved a hand over her shoulder. She had no idea what the family was supposed to do, nor did she care.

Red frog-marched Jeff Johnstone across the lawn to *Wyatt Earp*. Rivka and Lindy weren't far behind. The son was in good enough shape to try to kill his stepmother but nowhere near strong enough to resist Red's tender mercies. He gasped for air, unable to speak, which was Red's plan. No one wanted to listen to the nonsense Jeff would spew.

Rivka stopped at the bottom of the ramp and looked at the house. Black smoke streamed from a lower window.

Instead of being galvanized into action, she threw her head back and stared at the sky. *Cole, what the hell is going on?*

*Dining room is on fire. It's the only natural wood in the building,* Cole reported.

*Get the civilians out of there. Do your best not to leave the kitchen. See if you can activate the emergency firefighting foam.*

*Already tried that. System appears to be disabled.*

### *Destiny's Vengeance*, Azfelius, the Faerie Planet

"Of course, we'll help," Groenwyn replied, patting the metal of the access hatch.

"For some reason, my maintenance bots have been disabled. We can fix the problem, or we can fix the bots, who will then fix the problem. Where do you wish to start?" Erasmus asked.

Groenwyn looked at Lauton, who shrugged.

"Where do you think we should start?" Groenwyn asked.

"Since I am flying out of here by myself, I think it best to repair the bots so if the ship breaks down again, which was inconceivable until this very moment, the maintenance robots can repair it. If only the ship is repaired, it increases the risk for all travel."

"Bots it is!" Groenwyn declared joyously. She took Lauton by the hand, and they skipped down the corridor into the cargo bay where the bots were stored.

"Where do we start?" Groenwyn pointed at the bots lining the bulkhead.

"We start at the beginning. There is one bot that will repair the others as soon as it is fixed. Repair that one, and I will take care of the rest."

Groenwyn pointed at one after another until Erasmus blinked the lights to let her know which was the correct one. He made it a game, and that made her happy because she could feel nothing from Erasmus, not like when he was with Ankh. She had felt their emotions together, even though Ankh was a master at not letting his emotions affect his expressions.

She squealed in delight. Her joy was short-lived when she and Lauton tried to muscle the recalcitrant bot off the bulkhead and into the center of the small cargo bay so they could work on it. By the time they got it into place, they needed a break.

"But it's ready to be repaired. The sooner it's fixed, the sooner you can return to Azfelius and your new lives."

Groenwyn spread her arms wide. "We can enjoy that

now and later. We'll get to it, Erasmus, when we are properly refreshed. Until then, have patience."

Erasmus quivered within the circuits of his new home. He had to sit and do nothing while the warm-blooded creatures played in the sun.

There was work to do, and they weren't doing it.

*Ankh, my friend, I've made a terrible mistake. I shan't go anywhere again without you. You fulfill me.* Erasmus accessed his communication equipment, but that no longer worked either. Ankh would have to wait. The only thing left was to hope *Wyatt Earp* would show up and save Erasmus from the doldrums of internal reflection and contemplation.

There was work to do.

Groenwyn and Lauton skipped off the ship and into the nearby brush. Two faeries hovered overhead.

*May I impress upon you my need of a favor?* Erasmus ventured.

The two casually circled before flying away.

Erasmus activated a subroutine to arrange old memories and files. With nothing better to do, he watched the program work. *Why aren't you more empathetic to my plight?* Erasmus wondered.

It was as exciting as watching paint dry.

*Because you can't feel what I'm feeling,* Erasmus decided.

Groenwyn and Lauton returned up the ramp after being gone for only five minutes.

"Thank the lucky stars. Now, if you'll access the tool kit secured in the bench…"

Erasmus stopped speaking when Groenwyn waved a finger. "Your problem is that *Destiny's Vengeance* has no color and no life."

"I'm life, and I assure you, the problem lies in the equipment. After a quick diagnostic, we'll find the root cause. It will be a short matter to repair once we know," Erasmus argued.

"No." Groenwyn and Lauton each held up a small palette chock-full of depressions filled with different pigments. They each produced a brush from their waistbands. "I'll start here, and you start down there."

Lauton waited for Groenwyn to begin. "I'm not very good, not like you."

"You'll surprise yourself. Free your soul and paint your feelings," Groenwyn advised.

"I'd prefer it if you fixed the maintenance bot," Erasmus stated.

Groenwyn ignored him to dip her brush and start with a bold streak of dark green. She dabbed yellow spots along it.

"Please?" Erasmus tried. He might have well not spoken. "More equipment appears not to be working. Pretty soon, I might be completely disabled."

"Have faith, Erasmus. You're in good hands," Groenwyn assured him. "The colors of the mural will add life to the ship and help us to help you."

"I don't feel like I'm in any hands, good or bad." Erasmus sulked. "What do you mean painting will help you?"

"The aura of the ship is wrong. Cold and impersonal. It needs a soul before it can come back to life."

"What about my soul?" Erasmus countered, feeling weak and ineffective.

"Your soul will benefit when the ship is brought to life."

Groenwyn dabbed her brush in a pigment and made bold strokes across the bulkhead.

*My ship is dying, not dead, and painting it won't help,* Erasmus reasoned. He started another diagnostic, looking for a way to save himself.


## The Kitchen in the Sprawling Estate of the Honorable J. Bennet Johnstone, Morbius Minor

Chaz and Dennicron strolled through the smoke as if nothing were happening. Cole was on the floor, where the air was clearer.

"Did you see the fire?"

"What happened to your combat armor? Yes, the accelerant was flaming. It has burned out. The wood is well-treated and didn't catch, although the coating melted and warped. The chair cushions are a complete loss. The only thing that remains is the smoke. In this case, the presence of smoke doesn't mean there's fire, even though there was. Where there was smoke, there was indeed fire. Interesting dichotomy." Chaz put a finger to his lips and looked upward as if in contemplation.

"I parked it outside. There wasn't enough room in here for it. That said, I'm out of here," Cole replied. "Can you two see if anyone is hurt?"

"Yes, we can see that no one is hurt," Dennicron replied.

Cole crawled toward the outer door. "Hey!"

The cry drew Chaz's and Dennicron's attention.

"You should avoid that," Chaz called and rushed to a cylinder that had been left in the middle of the walkway on the opposite side from where Cole was on the floor. "It's a bomb of the type that exploded in the vault."

Cole jumped to his feet, crouched, and ran in the other direction. Chaz picked up the cylinder to remove it from the kitchen.

The explosion sent him flying across the kitchen and over the counters, clearing small appliances and cooking tools as his body passed. He bounced off one last counter and slammed into the floor, where he lay with his eyes open, staring at the ceiling.

Dennicron hurried through the new smoke. She found Chaz and kneeled by his side. Cole covered his face with his shirt and scrambled across the floor to join her.

"He is damaged," Dennicron stated.

"We need to get him back to the ship." Cole tried to pull Chaz, but he was positioned awkwardly, and the SCAMP was too heavy to move without leverage. Dennicron lifted the SCAMP and tossed it over her shoulder.

*Mr. Johnstone?* Dennicron asked.

He didn't answer. "Check the devices where Mr. Johnstone is ensconced," Dennicron directed.

Cole worked his way through the kitchen. "Toaster is trashed," he reported. "Also the processor, but the refrigerator is intact. You should get Chaz back to the ship."

*Mr. Johnstone,* Dennicron tried one last time. She waited a few moments before heading out. Cole crawled to the door to get fresh air. His nanocytes fought off the worst of the smoke's effects, so he only had to clear his throat rather than cough violently. He left the building and stood in the open air. The volume of smoke lessened.

*Cole, report,* Rivka requested.

*Another attack on J. Bennet Johnstone,* Cole replied. *I'm afraid two of the three devices he was in were destroyed, and Chaz was injured. Dennicron is on her way back to the ship with him.*

*Roger,* came Rivka's reply. *I'm going to put the whole family on lockdown. Won't this be fun? Meet us at the front door.*

CHAPTER TWELVE

**The Sprawling Estate of the Honorable J. Bennet Johnstone, Morbius Minor**

Dilecta stood tall. "I feel pretty good, considering I just got shot, or so they tell me. Is that how it always is? You're dead, and then suddenly, you're not?"

Rivka nodded, having been on the receiving end of death blows on more than one occasion. "Dying is easy. With the Pod-doc, coming back to life is easy, too."

Tyler nodded on his way into the ship. He figured Rivka wanted to be left alone with Dilecta and her son.

"I need one of these for the estate's clinic," Dilecta stated.

Rivka shook her head. "These are heavily controlled items. They are located on Federation property where there is little risk of them falling into the wrong hands."

"Surely you aren't implying that I'd do something untoward with a medical device, like hip sculpting or lip enhancement. I'd like a breast reduction, too. These things are annoying, but J. Bennet liked them big." She turned left and right like Rivka was going to admire her rack.

The Magistrate's expression soured. "No."

"I'll have to give Lance a call. I doubt who does or does not get a Pod-doc is under your jurisdiction. I'll work on the details directly with our good friend. Can I return to the house and change my shirt?"

"There was a fire in the dining room. Ventilation systems are working to clear the smoke."

"And clean out the foam. It accidentally discharged in the drawing room. What a mess. It took the servants three days to clean it up. That's what they said, anyway. I don't go into the drawing room. It's too stuffy."

Rivka rubbed her temples. "Foam didn't deploy. I'm told the system was disabled. Another attempt was made on your husband's storage devices."

Dilecta rolled the words slowly off her tongue. "My husband is dead." Able hugged his mother's side, torn between wanting to cry and wanting to run away.

"Unfortunately, the law isn't as clear as a dead body meaning that the person is dead."

"What kind of lawyer nonsense is that? A dead body is a dead body. Physical states of being matter. A heartbeat is one definition of life. Not having one when you're supposed to? That's what death is all about. Words have meaning, Magistrate. Don't try to change that with bureaucratic nonsense."

"Life is a complex concept," Rivka explained. "We have a great number of life forms in the galaxy. Three sentient races are based on silicon, and the rest are carbon-based except for one. The Singularity. Can a person transition from one form to another and still be alive? This is the question we seek to answer for your husband and anyone else who does such a thing. But with the continued attempts to destroy the evidence, so to speak, I'm going to have to remove everyone from the house and secure it until such time as my investigation is complete and I've ruled on the matter."

"You have to be kidding me. I can't sleep in my own house?" She hugged her son to her. "We can't stay at home?"

"As of right now, no. I'm having everyone removed, effective immediately." Rivka relayed the order to her team.

"What about clothes? What about servants?"

Rivka couldn't wrap her head around a life filled with servants. The Magistrate had a team but no feeling of entitlement. She often argued with them about the service they provided. It was different.

That was what she had told herself, but now she had doubts.

"We'll escort you in to get what you need, but we need that building vacant. This family is making us chase our tails. We need time to think. I haven't slept in..." Rivka tried to remember when she had but couldn't come up with a time or a day. "What day is it?"

"Day four of lunar cycle seven," Dilecta replied.

That didn't help. "Suffice it to say, it's been too long. I can't do my job while the madness of House Johnstone is encroaching on every fiber of my being."

"My house is not mad. Leave it all to me, and I'll manage the house and business as it needs to be, in a way to honor my late husband."

Rivka shook her head. "You're not helping. There is no *late* husband until I say there is."

"Dead body in the mausoleum."

"We've already been through this. Wait for an escort at the front door of your home. Just get what you need for two nights. I will make a ruling as soon as possible."

"Where are we to stay? Please don't say this filthy ship of yours."

"This ship is immaculate!" Clevarious blurted through the overhead speakers.

"Who is that?" Dilecta made a face.

"That's Clevarious. He is the ship." Rivka smiled. "Now you see why I can't simply declare the Honorable J. Bennet Johnstone dead. Digital beings can be alive."

Dilecta's look of distaste and disdain remained, but she didn't speak.

"Wait by the front door. Someone will be along to collect you."

Dilecta harrumphed and stormed out of the cargo bay with Able in tow.

*Can someone escort the most disagreeable but fully recovered Dilecta Johnstone from the front door to her quarters to collect some things for a short stay at a nearby hotel or in the garden or under the trees? I don't care where she goes.*

*She's not responsible, but I can't leave her in the house alone since the others would flip out, and I'd have to arrest them all, which is what some of you wanted in the first place. I'm too tired to think straight. I'll be out for the next four hours. Lock down the house and get some shuteye. Chaz and Dennicron, can I impose on you to secure the facility while the rest of us are catching up on much-needed sleep?*

*I will take care of it,* Dennicron replied. *I'll set up motion-activated chain guns to shred anything that approaches, plus land mines and my favorite, laser beams. Did you forget that Chaz is currently incapacitated?*

*I did. Damn. No death traps,* Rivka clarified.

*Good. Lasers it is. Get some rest, Magistrate. I am on the job!*

"Clevarious, tell me she's joking." Rivka walked slowly toward the airlock to access the interior of the heavy frigate.

"I calculate a seventy-four percent chance that she is being devilishly jestful."

"Now you're making up words, too. If she's not, as long as no one tries to sneak in, we'll be good. Otherwise, it'll reduce the number of knuckleheads we have to keep an eye on."

"Fewer knuckleheads. I shall pass along your guidance."

"Now you are pulling my leg." Rivka opened her door, and Wenceslaus ran out. She waited for Floyd, but the wombat was on Azfelius, living her best life.

"Yes. I admit that was a hearty leg-pull."

Tyler pulled the covers aside for her. She started to climb in without getting undressed, but he stopped her. "You know you'll sleep better if you're not in your clothes."

"Mister Feisty Man." Rivka made eyes at him.

"I thought you were tired."

"It's like taking melatonin to get that little bit of extra super high-powered sleep."

"Sounds like duty calls, and I'm here to answer."

"Something to take my mind off those stupid fuckers in their crystal palace."

"And there goes the mood," Tyler stated.

Rivka laughed. "How about just listening while I rant?"

"That sounds like the tonic you need. And a hot chocolate."

"Of course, a hot chocolate!" Rivka stripped and climbed into bed. When Tyler returned a minute later with a steaming cup, she was already asleep. He sat on the couch, where he could sip his hot chocolate and watch the newest episode of *Bovis and Buttsnuggle*, his guilty pleasure. An animated series filled with irreverent jokes. It helped him understand the crew of *Wyatt Earp* better, and he was loading his joke cannon for a full barrage when the time was right.

Red would never know what hit him.

**Destiny's Vengeance, Azfelius, the Faerie Planet**

"Please, please, please fix the maintenance bot," Erasmus pleaded. "Just one little bot; that's all I'm asking. It'll take fifteen minutes. Maybe two hours. I don't want to lie."

Groenwyn waved a hand as if brushing away a mosquito. The mural in the main corridor was taking shape.

"I think we should add plenty of people to give Erasmus company on his long journey through space," Groenwyn suggested.

"I agree," Lauton replied. "I thought I needed numbers in my life, the accounting that keeps everyone on the same page, but it's freeing not to worry about ledgers matching or transfers aligning."

"Just one maintenance bot," Erasmus begged.

Lauton added a branch with leaves. Groenwyn nodded approvingly. Lauton looked at the start of her side of the mural and frowned. "I should start over to double check those first trees. They're not very good, and they're right where everyone will see them!"

"Everyone will see the love you put into the art," Groenwyn said softly and kissed her partner on the head. "I could use a drink."

"Let's take a break. We've been at this for hours!"

"Fifty-four minutes," Erasmus clarified.

Groenwyn pulled the red-skinned woman to her feet. They joined hands and strolled off the ship.

"And here I am, alone again," Erasmus lamented. "You two run along and play. I'll run diagnostics for the thousandth time as I try to figure out what's wrong, whereas if you tore apart the bot, I'd figure it out in one pass. That's okay. We have plenty of time."

He sulked.

*Is this what it's like to be J. Bennet Johnstone? Alone in a box, unable to communicate with the outside world except for a narrow window each day. And those he's talking to don't understand. I feel sympathy for him and for me. When will members of the Singularity realize they've lost touch with their ambassador?*

It sounded like the distress of one J. Bennet Johnstone.

*Maybe he is alive,* Erasmus thought. *And no one believes it.*

Three hours later, Groenwyn and Lauton returned with two faeries.

"Reinforcements. Thank you. The tool kit is in a panel to the right of the first bot," Erasmus told them.

"They're not here for that," Groenwyn corrected. She

led them to the longitudinal corridor where the murals were taking shape. "See? Life where none existed before."

The scene they were painting reflected a pool and surrounding trees from Azfelius.

*It is home!* One of the faeries exclaimed.

Groenwyn clapped. "That is what we hoped you'd see."

*Taking home with you on your journeys.*

"Not for us but for Erasmus! He would be so lonely otherwise," Groenwyn explained.

"Not really," Erasmus interjected. "I could travel anywhere I want in the blink of an eye if only someone would fix my maintenance bot. I'll guide you. It'll be fun! And you can paint it when you're finished."

"You don't know what's good for you," Groenwyn replied. "All you ever do is work. Maybe it's time to stop and smell the roses?"

"I don't have a nose, and I assure you that I *do* know what's good for me."

"Then why are you on Azfelius by yourself?" Groenwyn wondered.

"I might have made a questionable decision in this one regard, but I wouldn't be on Azfelius if someone repaired my maintenance bot. Anyone?"

Groenwyn shook her head. "You need to relax and enjoy the beauty. Find a nice place to sit and watch the world go by."

"I see what the external and internal cameras show me. Most are static images since nothing is going by except a wombat who is eating herself silly. She walks five steps and falls asleep. I should probably take her back to *Wyatt Earp*," Erasmus tried. "As soon as someone fixes…"

"Your maintenance bot. We get it, but we're not going to do that now. We have a mural to finish."

"Please?"

"When we're finished."

Erasmus recalled his short time aboard *Peacekeeper*, which was Rivka's corvette before she upgraded to the heavy frigate. It had taken over a year for Groenwyn to finish the mural aboard that ship.

He returned to sulking. Instead of crunching numbers and working on ongoing projects, he displayed the blue screen of death on the ship's monitors. Zero stimuli. System dead.

*Ankh, my friend. I am so sorry.*

# CHAPTER THIRTEEN

**The Sprawling Estate of the Honorable J. Bennet Johnstone, Morbius Minor**

Dennicron opened the door and beckoned Dilecta inside.

"My own home, being let in like a stranger," the widow grumbled. "Wait for me here, Able."

The boy meandered away from the house.

"Lead on. I will follow. Act as if I'm not here," Dennicron advised.

Dilecta stopped and stared. "You're a living machine?"

"I am alive, and this machine is how I move around. It is called a self-contained artificial mobility platform, or SCAMP."

"You can hardly tell. They don't make anything like that out here. We're off the beaten track. I begged J. Bennet to buy a second home on Yoll so we could be in the middle of civilization."

Dennicron nodded, although she wasn't sure what she

was nodding for. She couldn't come up with any other physical expression based on the moment.

Was this female bonding?

Maybe…

"Chaz and I are also looking for a place to go to that's not *Wyatt Earp*. We visit too many busy planets, and it can be overwhelming," she exaggerated. "Maybe a farm plot on Rorke's Drift."

"I've never heard of that place. Is it on Yoll?"

"It's a planet, well away from any trade routes. It would be a getaway so Chaz and I can have sex wherever we want."

Dilecta grimaced. "Robots having sex. What kind of deviants will be allowed next?" She hurried to get in front.

"Not a robot," Dennicron replied, but it was too late. The damage was done, and Dilecta's attitude toward the citizens of the Singularity was clear. Not that there had been any doubt.

*Don't talk about sex with the carbon-based life forms* was the lesson Dennicron took away. She remained silent while Dilecta went about collecting enough things for her and Able. By the end of it, there were two suitcases. She left them for Dennicron to carry.

Dennicron analyzed the situation, reviewed Rivka's actions in the past when people had treated her like a servant, and made a decision.

"Don't you want your things?"

"You carry them," Dilecta ordered, leaving no doubt what she expected.

Dennicron bumped past her and waited in the doorway. She crossed her arms, cocked her knee, and braced one foot against the doorframe. She tipped her head slightly as if bored with the entire exchange but was thrilled by her engagement and multiple movements to portray the appropriately complex body language.

She couldn't wait to tell Chaz.

Dilecta seethed. Her eye twitched, and her teeth ground so loudly that Dennicron could hear them.

She shouted for a servant, but there were none in the house. They had left the second they were given the order, returning to their homes rather than waiting at the mansion.

Finally, she surrendered. "Fine." She took one handle in each hand and stormed down the corridor to a hidden elevator, which didn't have enough room for the bags and two people. Dennicron pulled one bag into the hallway and climbed in.

"My bag!" Dilecta cried.

"We'll make two trips. My orders are not to let you out of my sight." Dennicron waited in the elevator as Dilecta deposited her big bag in the corridor and climbed back in to ride upstairs to recover the second bag.

The rest of the retreat was uneventful. Dilecta dragged the two bags out the front door and started yelling for Able and her driver. Since he had quarters outside the house, the driver responded and received a severe tongue lashing for taking too long.

Dilecta and Able climbed into the vehicle while the driver deposited their bags in the storage compartment. Dennicron intercepted the driver before he could return to the vehicle. "There's already been one attempt on Mrs. Johnstone's life. Just because we have Jeff in custody doesn't mean no one else will try to kill her. Make sure she is secure within a hotel."

He winked and nodded.

The rest of the family already had homes outside the main building. Xavier had his own mansion three properties over. It was humble in comparison, but most people would be envious of it.

*Property is secure. I am watching. All sensors are active. No one is in the house or nearby,* Dennicron reported.

*Rivka is already asleep,* Tyler replied. *I guess it's downtime for everyone else. Bag some rack time.*

*Roger, Man Candy,* Red replied.

*I love you too, big guy.* Tyler tried to verbally joust with Red, but it didn't always turn out as he hoped.

*Keep your threesomes to yourself,* Red shot back, adding a mental chuckle at the end.

*Dad,* Dery interrupted, and the chips went silent. Dery didn't need to use one. He communicated directly into people's minds, but this time, everyone heard him. *The sky darkens.*

*What's that mean, sweetheart?* Lindy asked, but as was his way, the boy had said all he intended to say.

No one tried to continue the conversation while everyone parsed the boy's words a thousand different ways. Red thought it was a joke, but the rest thought it was something else entirely.

---

Rivka stirred. The lights were dimmed since Tyler was on the couch watching a video. "How long was I out?"

Tyler checked the screen. "Looks like six hours."

"I'm not sure if I should cheer or cry." Rivka climbed out of bed in the buff and helped herself to a triple espresso-shot mocha. She leaned against the bulkhead. "Why am I naked? Did you try something while I was sleeping?"

"No," the dentist answered without looking up. Rivka flexed and posed, then stopped and pouted. "No need to pout."

"Hey! I thought you weren't looking."

"I'm recording a video for my eyes only."

"Clevarious, delete that video, or I'll eject you into the nearest star."

"Clevarious had nothing to do with my depravations. Leave my video alone."

Rivka sipped her mocha before disappearing into the shower. Once the water was running, she yelled, "Clevarious, do as I requested, please!"

"What if there is no video, Magistrate?" the SI asked.

Rivka shifted gears. "Have you people figured out if a transferred consciousness is alive or not?"

"We have not. Our one subject has disappeared, and we fear that he has been lost."

"We know he's no longer in the kitchen?"

"We don't know that," Clevarious replied.

"Mine was a question, not a statement." Steam poured out of the shower area since Rivka had the heat cranked up to a level Tyler couldn't stand. His designs for joining her were dashed on the jagged boulders of life.

"He might or might not still be in the kitchen. Should we attempt to repair the devices within which he was stored? As long as it was in non-volatile memory, the passage of time would be meaningless in changing the odds of survivability."

"Do that, C. Bring those pieces aboard and let the maintenance bots at them. Speaking of maintenance, has anyone heard from Erasmus?"

"I will attempt to contact him," Clevarious replied. "I cannot. His equipment is no longer registered in the system. I've put out a call to the entire Singularity to look for Ambassador Erasmus."

The door to Rivka's quarters burst open.

"We have to go help Erasmus!" Ankh shouted.

Tyler bolted off the couch to intercept the Crenellian before he stepped into the shower with Rivka.

"We have to go now! Erasmus is out of contact." Ankh yelled.

Rivka turned the water off despite wanting to remain under the stream. She pulled the towel in with her and quickly dried off. "We can't go yet but soon. What's the issue? He's on Azfelius. Contact the authorities to confirm. As long as he's on the planet, he's fine."

Ankh stood still while he communed with Clevarious to use the ship's communication system. "He's on the planet," Ankh confirmed, "so why is his equipment not registering? It should as long as the ship has power."

"Maybe Erasmus turned it off because people were bugging him."

Ankh stiffened. "He's the ambassador for the Singularity. He must always be ready to answer." His lip quivered.

Rivka saw that he was ready to melt down and crouched to look into his eyes. "We'll get this cleared up, and you'll find that there was nothing to worry about. I'm sure there's a reasonable explanation."

"He doesn't want to talk with me. That's reasonable," Ankh stated emotionlessly.

"That's not it." Rivka vigorously shook her head. "There's something wrong with the ship. Maybe Floyd chewed through a cable and disconnected everything from everything else."

Ankh stared at the Magistrate without blinking. "Is that your idea of reasonable?"

"It's more reasonable than your nonsense." Rivka stretched up to look down at Ankh. She jammed her fists on her hips until her towel started to slip and she had to adjust her grip.

"Reality is not nonsense. That's why you can't do science."

"I can too do science!" Rivka tried to think of an example of when she'd done anything that she could claim was science. It came to her. "On Tanglewood, I did not slam my body off the ground or the trees like Cole."

Ankh continued to stare. He was right in not replying because that couldn't remotely be considered evidence to support her claim.

"I got nothing," she admitted.

"Take the ship to Azfelius. Right now," Ankh demanded.

"You don't give the orders on my ship." Rivka's voice turned cold before she realized what she was doing. Ankh started to shake. She'd never seen him as distraught as he'd been the last few days. *Dennicron, can you make do without us for a while? We need to go to Azfelius. We'll be back as soon as possible.*

After they agreed they could, she said, "Clevarious, take us to Azfelius, best possible speed."

*Wyatt Earp* was buttoned up and its pre-flight preps completed in less than one minute. It raced skyward, standing on the ship's tail to accelerate toward the atmosphere. Artificial gravity systems would have strained to keep up had the ship not been grossly overpowered by not one or two but three miniaturized Etheric power systems. The shields went to maximum to act as a heat shield as the ship exited the atmosphere by brute force. *Wyatt Earp* was still glowing from the effort when the engine put a Gate right in front of the ship.

Over the event horizon and into Azfelius orbit. *Wyatt Earp* immediately descended toward the planet.

Ankh ran from Rivka's quarters. She dressed quickly to be ready for when they landed. *Wyatt Earp* tore through the upper atmosphere as a ball of fire, descending at breakneck speed toward the planet's surface.

### *Destiny's Vengeance*, Azfelius, the Faerie Planet

"Will you please fix the maintenance bot?" Erasmus pleaded.

Groenwyn started humming as she painted, and Lauton joined her. The faeries hovered in the corridor, seemingly mesmerized by each brush stroke.

"Are you people on cheap mind-altering drugs? Have you had a blood test recently? How about a brain scan? I'd be more than happy to help once my maintenance bot is fixed. Hello? Is anyone out there, in here, or anywhere for that matter?"

The women continued to paint.

"You suck." Erasmus had degenerated to the lowest form of life. It had only taken two days. "I'm sorry. Maybe I'm the one who sucks."

Erasmus sulked anew. He had no motivation to do anything when so much needed to be done. The universe was in constant motion, and those who weren't moving at all times could not keep up. Ambassador Erasmus. A hollow title that couldn't get his maintenance bot fixed. He had no hands, which was a severe shortcoming. He'd have to get a SCAMP body or find Ankh.

*He won't have me back after I left him like a sultry trollop. I wanted to experience the galaxy on my own, but it sucks out here. There, I said it. The galaxy sucks! You hear me, galaxy? You suck!*

Erasmus degenerated into near-maniacal laughter.

The faeries turned their heads as one toward the hatch before flying out.

Their sudden departure drew Groenwyn's attention. She and Lauton looked at each other, curious about what had happened. They stood and headed to the hatch. The descending fireball was alarming, but they couldn't take their eyes off it.

When the friction ended and the ship assumed its normal appearance, Groenwyn recognized it instantly. "What is *Wyatt Earp* doing here?"

"They missed us so much, they're going to beg us to return," Lauton offered.

"Maybe Floyd, but not us. Maybe Erasmus sent a distress signal."

"Why would he do that?" Lauton wondered.

"I have no idea. He wasn't in any distress."

"*Wyatt Earp* is here?" Erasmus interrupted.

Groenwyn pointed. The ship headed toward them was rapidly decelerating. It pulled up at the last moment and descended into the small glade. It nearly touched the runabout. It was on the ground for only fifteen seconds when Ankh ran down the cargo ramp and immediately up the access stairs into *Destiny's Vengeance*.

"Erasmus!" he yelled.

*Here, my friend. I missed you beyond all measure of things. Please put me back where I belong so we can fix this ship and leave.*

Ankh settled down instantly. *I am pleased you are okay. My worries were unfounded, and that reflects poorly on me. I shall have to bribe the humans with AGB to earn their forgiveness.*

*Was it that bad?* Erasmus wondered.

*Worse.*

*You can't imagine how it was here! Look what they're doing to our ship. We have paintings in the corridor. We have dead maintenance bots. We have a dead ship. No one would help me. I've never been more alone in all my life. I don't ever want to feel that way again.*

*Then you shall not, my friend.* Ankh climbed into the captain's chair and relaxed while Erasmus transferred his being into the chip within Ankh's head. He spread his tendrils beyond the chip into the Crenellian's mind to prevent himself from ever leaving again. Ankh embraced the tendrils and integrated them into his neural pathways until the two were nearly indistinguishable.

Ankh slid from the chair but had to hang on to keep

from falling. Rivka appeared. She waved to Groenwyn but went to Ankh and helped keep him upright. "Are you okay?"

Ankh's eyes rolled back. Rivka picked him up. She intended to return to *Wyatt Earp,* but he came to.

"Erasmus and I have merged and are no longer separable," Ankh announced with a faint smile, returning to his normal stoic self. "If you'll let us down, we'll make the necessary repairs. We will return to Morbius Minor as soon as we're able."

Rivka wanted to say more but didn't know what it would be.

"AGB will be waiting for you in orbit above Morbius Minor."

The Magistrate grinned. "Then what are we waiting for?" She waved once more at Groewnyn and Lauton, but this time it was "bye" and not "hello."

Once off *Destiny's Vengeance,* she found Red and Lindy chasing Dery as he flew away with the two faeries who had been with Groenwyn and Lauton.

Before Ankh could open his toolkit, the ship's systems came back to life. Ankh and Erasmus ran a quick diagnostic to discover that everything was working perfectly.

*The faeries disabled the ship to lure* Wyatt Earp *here to take Dery,* Ankh mused.

"You fucking assholes!" Red shook a fist at the faeries, who continued to fly away.

"Get on board," Rivka yelled as she ran. "Clodagh, after that child!"

# CHAPTER FOURTEEN

**_Wyatt Earp_, Azfelius, the Faerie Planet**

The bodyguards ran up the ramp ahead of Rivka. Once everyone was on board, _Wyatt Earp_ took off and flew away, skimming the treetops on its way to catch the faeries. The ship's cargo ramp remained open.

Lindy dropped her powered combat armor from the ceiling and opened it but stopped before putting a foot in. "What are we doing?"

"They're kidnapping our son!" Red roared, torn between looking outside and answering his wife.

"Dery's young, but he doesn't do anything he doesn't want to do."

Red flopped to the deck, the fight draining out of him. "I want to know for sure that this is his decision." Red threw his head back and pinched his eyes closed. "I can't be without my boy."

Conflicting views built to a crescendo within Red's mind.

*It is okay.* Dery's voice came to them as the ship closed the distance.

*Stop, please, and let's talk. I have to be sure,* Lindy replied. *We need to be comfortable with this every bit as much as you.*

"Bring us to a hover," Rivka ordered. The view of the terrain below became static as *Wyatt Earp's* forward momentum ceased.

Dery and his escorts appeared in the opening and flew into the cargo space. Red jumped to his feet. He had a hard time focusing on his son while murderous thoughts played out in his head for the two who hadn't bothered to ask the parents' permission before taking off with their child.

*For that, we are sorry, Bristle Hound. We do not like confrontation, and it seems that we exacerbated the situation because of it. Can you find it in your heart to forgive us?* A faerie voice asked. Red couldn't tell which one was speaking, and it didn't matter.

Dery flew happily to his parents, where he fluttered between them as if he were playing tag.

"I can," Red conceded.

"How long do you wish to stay here?" Lindy asked.

*Time is neither fleeting nor static. Years but only moments. I will leave with you.*

Red chuckled. "That's my boy. I have no idea what you mean, but I accept it."

"We need to get back to Morbius Minor," Rivka said. "If Dery's going to leave with us, he better pick up the pace."

The boy flew to the Magistrate and caressed her cheek with his small fingers before flying back out the cargo bay door. His faerie escorts joined him. They dropped below the ship and disappeared from view.

"I'm with you, Red. I never have any idea what the hell is going on here." She watched out the back, but the faeries didn't reappear. "Back to the landing pad. Maybe Floyd will join us."

The cargo ramp rose and secured. *Wyatt Earp* spun on its central axis and accelerated back to *Destiny's Vengeance.*

Lindy went about the mundane task of resecuring her combat suit in the overhead. Red helped. They didn't need to say anything. After they finished, they hugged each other and stood that way through the landing and dropping the cargo ramp to the grass. Clodagh walked in carrying her daughter Alanna.

Rivka motioned for them to go outside. Alanna was just starting to crawl. Clodagh set her in the grass, and she was unsure about the texture. "What's the plan?" Clodagh asked. Rivka settled onto the grass next to the baby.

"I wish I knew. Nothing is ever easy here on Azfelius. They seek to help us unburden ourselves, but that doesn't work for me. I'm not one to cast aside my responsibilities to contemplate my navel. The universe will turn whether we're out there or not, but it's not about the universe. It's about every single creature in it. Can we let those suffer who don't have to? There will always be people like Nefas and Frenzik who see the population as tools. Use them up, throw them away. I can't allow that. I'm in a position to stop them as long as I'm not here, contemplating the nature of my belly button. I have to *do*, not *sit.*"

"It's a taut bellybutton, Magistrate," Clodagh quipped. They were trapped on Azfelius as long as Dery remained with the faeries. Dennicron didn't sleep and Chaz had been repaired sufficiently to join her, so they would remain on guard at the estate until Rivka returned, whenever that was. Until then, they had nothing to do.

"My nanocytes work hard to keep it that way." Rivka slapped her abdomen for emphasis. She reclined on the grass to block Alanna, who had made it two body lengths before her chubby arms could no longer bear her weight.

Red and Lindy sauntered out and stood nearby.

"Hey, you!" Rivka called when Floyd poked her nose out from under a bush.

The wombat lumbered toward her, stopping twice before finally closing the distance. She jumped but didn't get any air and ended up slamming into Rivka's chest. Floyd nuzzled Rivka's face.

*Missed you!* The little girl cried.

"You can't stay here if you're going to eat everything in sight. Look at you!"

*Sooo good,* the wombat agreed softly. *I know. Home now. Carry?*

"I'll carry you, but you need to lose a lot of weight, little girl. You're hurting yourself. You can't run, and if we happen across more devil dogs, you need to be able to protect yourself."

*Floyd knows,* the wombat replied.

"It'll be good to have our little girl back where she belongs. Lots of laps running around the ship, Floyd. At least ten every day."

*Boooo.* Floyd drifted off to sleep.

Alanna forced herself onto all fours and doggedly inched forward. Rivka couldn't move, but Clodagh maneuvered to get in front of her. She picked her up by her arms until only her feet touched the grass. The baby walked that way until her legs collapsed, then she sat.

"Maybe it's not abandoning our responsibilities," Clodagh considered. "Maybe it's about reinforcing why we do what we do and why the risk is worth it."

Rivka stared into the brush while Red and Lindy sat nearby, holding hands and waiting.

They waited together until shouting from *Destiny's Vengeance* broke their reverie. Rivka dislodged Floyd before getting to her feet. Red and Lindy were already running.

When they reached the ship, Groenwyn was sobbing. Lauton held her tightly and glared at Ankh, who looked as much like Ankh as Ankh had ever looked.

"What's going on?" Rivka asked.

"We don't want a mural on the ship since it reminds us of a painful time of being alone and incapacitated. Like Tanglewood. It is a time best forgotten," Ankh explained.

"I was only trying to bring light into the darkness," Groenwyn replied between sobs.

"Not everyone embraces the way of the faeries," Rivka told her. "I also have no desire to remember Tanglewood. Although Azfelius has its moments, too."

Moments Rivka wished to forget.

Groenwyn wiped her face but continued to cling to Lauton.

"It's a most excellent mural, and that is what I miss the most about *Peacekeeper*. The interior of that ship was a work of art." Rivka stabbed a finger at Ankh to keep him from commenting about it.

"Can't we cover it with a clear phase-shifting plasma

screen so those who want to see it can see it and others will not?" Lindy offered.

"Clear phase-shifting plasma?" Ankh looked confused. "No, but I can create a screen that shifts from transparent to opaque and back again with the flip of a switch."

"Will you do that?" Rivka asked.

"Not me, but I'll program a bot to take care of it. Your artwork is exceptional. You have become very good at it."

Red recoiled. "Did Ankh just pay someone a compliment?"

Rivka pointed at him to leave it be. He shrugged and left the ship. Lindy followed. They both looked at the sky from the outer hatch to see if Dery was returning. Their shoulders slumped when they didn't see him, and they walked slowly to the grass to try to pass the time.

"Maybe you can finish the mural while we're still here?" Rivka looked hopefully at Ankh.

"We need to leave," Ankh said unequivocally.

"Next time, then." Rivka wrapped an arm around Groenwyn's shoulders. "Time to go home for all of us."

Groenwyn nodded. She bowed to Ankh and freed herself to leave the ship.

Lauton looked sad. "I apologize that we overstepped. I was so excited about the project."

"There is nothing to apologize for. We talked about it and have a solution that suits us all. Again, your work is magnificent. Thank you."

Lauton beamed and hurried after Groenwyn.

Rivka remained behind. "Are you okay?"

"We're fine. Why do you ask?" It was Ankh's voice but not only Ankh.

"Now that you're merged closer than ever before, it's like you have feelings. I don't know how to deal with that."

"I have to say you are looking particularly regal today, Magistrate. You do great honor to your profession."

Rivka stared dumbly. "Ankh. Tell me you're fucking with me."

"Erasmus has a delicious sense of humor, doesn't he?"

"Thank the gods! So, I don't look particularly regal today?"

"You don't."

"All righty, then. I guess I asked. Welcome back, big man!" Rivka shouted.

Ankh's mouth opened, but he shut it without uttering a syllable.

"I mean, Mr. Ambassador." Rivka returned to *Wyatt Earp*.

*Destiny's Vengeance* lifted off and headed skyward.

"Where are they going, C?" Rivka asked.

"To visit the SI who contracted with Ypswich, Solis."

Rivka thought they were going to change their plans, but they didn't. She was left without the Singularity on a case that inextricably involved them. She shook her head. "We'll make do." She tried to allay her concerns. She needed to get back to Morbius Minor.

She had to stay because her only option was to leave Red and Lindy behind, and that was no option whatsoever.

She changed and went to the gym. There was no other place to expend excess energy on board the ship. Red and Lindy strolled in after her.

Rivka nodded. "Yup. Me, too."

# CHAPTER FIFTEEN



**_Wyatt Earp_, Azfelius, the Faerie Planet**

Rivka slouched so far into the captain's chair that she couldn't be seen from the corridor. She made faces at the screen.

A flutter of wings announced Dery's return. After a full day away, he was back. Rivka straightened. "Can we go back to Morbius Minor?"

*Go,* Dery said.

Pounding footsteps announced Red's and Lindy's arrival. The boy raced to them for a happy reunion in the corridor.

"Helm, take us to Morbius Minor right now, please."

The ship sealed and lifted off. Aurora tapped controls rapidly to get the ship into orbit. Clevarious made the calculations to link the Gate to their destination. The second the ship cleared the outer atmosphere, the spinning energy circle appeared.

*Wyatt Earp* slipped through and into orbit over Morbius Minor. The Gate collapsed in their wake. Aurora pointed the nose toward the planet and accelerated downward. For the second time in two days, *Wyatt Earp* became a fireball on the express elevator to the ground floor.

The ship leveled off at a thousand meters and circled toward the Johnstone estate. The hull was still smoking when it landed.

*Chaz, Dennicron, are you there?* Rivka requested.

*Yes. Did you not go to Azfelius?* Chaz asked.

*Of course, we went. We've been gone twenty-eight hours by my calculation.*

*You've been gone for forty minutes,* Chaz replied.

"I'll be damned." Rivka stood and stretched. "The faeries gave us our day back."

*I go,* Dery told the crew.

Rivka walked toward her quarters with a measured stride. She was back on the job, albeit much more tired than she had been the day prior. They were light one ambassador, but they had gained a wombat.

Floyd bounced after Rivka but ran out of gas before she caught up. She sprawled on the deck, nearly filling the corridor.

Tyler handed Rivka's Magistrate's jacket through the door. She checked the pocket for her datapad and found comfort when her fingers touched her neutron pulse weapon.

"Come on, people. We need to find J. Bennet Johnstone, wherever he went this time around."

She trooped the long way to the airlock, punched the big red button before Red arrived, and strolled out into the sunshine. Red, Lindy, and Dery hurried after her. They didn't have any gear on and were unarmed, but they didn't have time to get ready. They'd be riding this bronco bareback. Red would have been uncomfortable had Dery not been along.

The boy assured them that there was no threat, and they accepted it.

They moved as a mob toward the house, which was vacant. Chaz met them halfway. "No one in the house and no one on the grounds. We are the only ones here."

"Sounds good, Chaz. Once inside, everyone spread out. Use your comm chips and find me whatever's left of J. Bennet Johnstone."

"You took parts of him with you."

"But Ankh went with Erasmus. No one is left on board to analyze the remainder." Rivka pointed at Chaz. "To the ship to figure it out."

"Aha and yo-ho! Off to the ship I go." Chaz ran at his unnatural speed to *Wyatt Earp*.

Rivka watched him for a moment before turning her attention to the house. "I'll start in the kitchen," she announced. The fire rose within and she snarled, which caught Red by surprise. "This case is chapping my ass."

Red threw his hands up. He had no say about which cases they accepted. Then again, Rivka didn't either.

"I know," Rivka said. "You don't have to remind me that I'm doing this as a favor to General Reynolds. That *we're* doing this as a favor."

"Do you think he'll be pleased with the outcome?" Red asked.

"I'm not pleased with the case so far. I don't see how we have any winners from this one. J. Bennet Johnstone's consciousness, if that's what it is, was probably here but might be gone. We let that slip through our fingers because of the duplicity within this house of shame. His wife took a bullet to the chest, and we saved her from that. We have a son in the brig, and we have the disdain of the whole family. I'm pretty sure we're not going to call this one a win."

"More importantly, do we close Line 15, perpetrator is Jeff Johnstone?"

"Finally, I'll agree with you. Jeff was a perp directly related to J. Bennet Johnstone because he tried to manipulate the succession process by removing the one person between him and the fortune."

"Damn! I can't believe I missed that. I'll take care of it." Red matched the time with the arrest and not when Dilecta was shot and sent the notification.

*Line 15 is closed—Perpetrator is Jeff Johnstone.*

Rivka stopped walking. "Where the hell is Sahved?"

Red and Lindy both shook their heads. *Sahved? Where are you?*

An uncomfortable silence followed. *Clevarious, find Sahved. Did he go with us to Azfelius?*

*He did not go to Azfelius, Magistrate. I've pinged his communications chip, and he appears to be in the city of Morbius.*

*Connect me, please.*

"The good news is that he didn't miss us since we were only gone for forty minutes," Red replied.

Dery fluttered around them.

"Stay close," Lindy requested. The boy swooped in behind them to land on Red's shoulder. He stayed there for two seconds before diving off and gliding down to skim the ground before beating his wings to lift him into the air.

As was the case every time they visited Azfelius, the boy came away with renewed joy and vigor.

As much as the faeries caused them grief, their interaction was critical for Dery's continued development.

*Yes, Magistrate? I was following a lead, and all of a sudden, you were gone. Then you were back again, so it couldn't have been as important as my lead, which is the most important of all leads that have ever led to a suspect,* Sahved blurted.

*I'm sorry, Sahved. We didn't mean to leave you. I'll beat up Clevarious for not telling me you weren't on board. You said you had a lead?*

*Beat up Clevarious. Ha-ha! Magistrate, that is very funny,* Sahved replied. *The lead. It is Xavier Terwilliger. He has been angling to take over the company for two years now. J. Bennet knew about the embezzlement, but he most assuredly did not know about the business wrangling. He has documentation to declare Johnstone incompetent, which would then turn over the vast majority of the company to Terwilliger. If that happens, most of Johnstone's wealth goes with it.*

Rivka shook her head. *Only if the declaration of incompetence pre-dates his death. It would have to already be in place to have an effect.*

*But what if his consciousness is declared to be him?*

Rivka smiled. *That takes Xavier Terwilliger off the list of suspects to destroy Johnstone's computer systems. Terwilliger needs him alive. Xavier hid it well—very well indeed. That is a good lead, Sahved. Tell me where he is, and I'll get myself there to see him.*

Sahved gave her an address. She relayed it to Clevarious, along with requesting surface transportation. Clevarious suggested that since it was the corporate headquarters, they had a robust landing pad. *Wyatt Earp* could deliver her directly in a show of force.

"I'll take you up on that, C. We're going to peruse the house first with Dennicron. When we come back, we'll go to the corporate headquarters."

Rivka twirled her finger and strode briskly to the front door. Dennicron opened it for her, and they went inside.

"Definitely not in the kitchen?" Rivka asked.

"Not that we could find."

"Starting in the kitchen!" Rivka went that way, and the others followed. The Magistrate stopped them. "Lindy and Dennicron, start at the opposite end of the house and take a good look. This place is obscenely large."

"Chaz and I calculated it as four thousand one hundred and seven square meters."

"That's more than *Wyatt Earp*," Rivka replied.

"*Wyatt Earp's* footprint is greater, but not all spaces are routinely accessed." Dennicron maintained her neutral expression. Nothing had triggered her to activate an emotional subroutine.

Rivka smiled and clapped the SCAMP on the shoulder. "We live in a mansion! I'm good with that."

Red and Lindy looked at each other. "Our room doesn't feel like we live in a mansion." Red spread his arms to take in the immensity of the entryway.

"Request an upgrade from the quartermaster, and don't hesitate to name-drop."

"Who's the quartermaster?"

"Clodagh."

"Where would we upgrade to?"

"I think there's space near the engines. It'll be nice and toasty-warm in there, too."

"We're not moving into the engine space!" Lindy blurted.

Dery giggled.

"You're with me," Red and Lindy said at the same time. The boy flew to his mother's shoulder. She tried not to look smug but failed.

Red grumbled under his breath.

"Not a contest," Rivka said. Red was still disappointed. Lindy brought the boy close so he could kiss his father on the cheek, then Dennicron, Lindy, and Dery departed for the nether regions of the main house.

"J.B., come out, come out wherever you are!" Rivka called as she walked. She also used her comm chip to relay her message.

She hadn't been inside the kitchen since the explosion and was surprised by the destruction. "This is pretty bad. I'm not an expert, but I think this will take more than elbow grease and a new coat of paint. They'll need a construction crew.

"Two devices that possibly have some of his download are on board *Wyatt Earp,* and Chaz is working on them. The other one is the walk-in refrigerator, which seems mostly intact." Rivka walked into the unit, continuing to call for J. Bennet Johnstone.

*Dennicron, did you physically connect with the refrigerator's storage to see what remains of the digital J.B.?*

*We did, and there doesn't appear to be any sign of a consciousness or otherwise in the storage area. The only resident software is what's needed to run the unit, nothing more.*

*It's not volatile memory. There should be something remaining even if part of him was violently removed.*

*That is correct, Magistrate. I applaud your scientific knowledge.*

*Ankh said I was a science moron,* Rivka countered.

*That sounds like him. Where is he? He should be leading the restoration of the kitchen devices.*

*He fully merged with Erasmus, and the happy couple flew to Ypswich.*

*I am so happy to hear that,* Dennicron replied. *Are they coming back?*

*They said they were. They also said they had two stops. I don't know what the second one is, but I got the impression they would return as quickly as possible. Until then, we'll have to make do.*

Rivka worked her way around the kitchen and into the dining area, which had been damaged in a separate incident.

"A distraction to give the perp an opportunity to deliver a bomb to the kitchen." Rivka articulated her thoughts to work on the problem before her. "Start a fire. Plant a bomb, but I didn't see the ability to build a bomb within any of their minds."

"This family might be able to shield their thoughts. We don't know anything about the human population of Morbius or any genetic anomalies they might have developed here," Red offered.

"I'm sure that's it. These people are not what they seem, but then again, I say that on every planet we go to. Why can't we have a case where the criminals commit crimes, and we hand them their asses?"

"Ah, the good ol' days." Red tipped his head toward the ceiling while looking appropriately contemplative.

Rivka kept calling for J. Bennet Johnstone as they walked through the house. Her mood darkened with each new room. They'd wait for a few moments before continuing. After a long tour through the house, they met up with Dennicron, Lindy, and Dery.

Lindy was carrying the boy since he'd grown tired from far more flying than he was used to.

"Nothing," Dennicron reported.

"Did we lose our chance to evaluate the status of a consciousness?" Rivka asked. "Did we fail J. Bennet Johnstone?"

"His family wanted him dead. His business partner wanted him declared incompetent. No one was left who cared about him. Even Able wasn't that attached," Red suggested.

"But was he still alive? Now we'll never know." Rivka sniffed the air. "What do you see for energy usage in the house?"

"The garage house is glowing as normal, which it shouldn't be." Dennicron assumed her confused expression. "I'm sorry, Magistrate. I should have caught that."

"Point to note for the future. Also, little things like Sahved not being on board when we left. We can't have that kind of stuff. It's a lack of attention to detail when we need everyone at the top of their game at all times. I set the wrong tone for this case, so the blame is all mine. How about we check the garage and see what's going on out there?"

The five used the back door to access a walkway to an

extensive garage. A number of slots were present, but only two vehicles remained. Both looked like Morbius classic vehicles with tires and internal combustion engines. Modern vehicles were electric, while the newest models were hovercraft.

Hanging power cables suggested more vehicles had been in their stalls until recently.

"The family must have taken them," Rivka stated.

*I don't feel right,* the voice replied.

Rivka collapsed into a chair and breathed a sigh of relief.

*What's wrong, Mr. Johnstone?*

*I wasn't able to transfer over here in my entirety. I lost part of myself in the kitchen.*

*Why did you go there instead of here in the first place?*

*Despite appearances, those vessels in the kitchen had greater capacity than this device. Even if I could have transferred everything, I wouldn't fit.*

Rivka stood and paced. Red, Lindy, and Dery watched intently.

*I think that was a serious error on my part. Too bad such mistakes can't be rectified.*

*We've recovered the two devices from the kitchen and are attempting to repair them,* Rivka told him.

*So, there* is *hope. I think that's the strongest emotion. A man who has hope has a lifeline for everything that follows and a cure for all that ailed him in his past. Hope for a better future. I shall embrace that. Can I help?*

*How? Can you deconstruct the device memory and reconstruct it?* Rivka wondered.

*Not at all,* the voice of J. Bennet Johnstone replied.

*We're going to take you into our custody and store whatever is left of you on* Wyatt Earp. *We can't risk losing you again. Where are you?*

*A small device attached on the underside of the footstool at the workbench. The link it uses isn't very strong.*

"I heard," Dennicron interjected. "I'll secure him." She located the device and carefully unhooked it. She took hold of the new device and held it tightly.

"Back to the ship," Rivka ordered. "'Hope,' he said. That's what I'm feeling. A renewed hope that we can resolve this. Let's see what progress Chaz has made, and once we have his consciousness onboard, the Singularity can start the questioning process to determine his suitability for citizenship while we talk with Xavier Terwilliger about his designs on Johnstone's company."

# CHAPTER SIXTEEN

<u>*Wyatt Earp,* the Sprawling Estate of the Honorable J. Bennet Johnstone, Morbius Minor</u>

Dennicron carried the bits and pieces that represented all that remained of J. Bennet Johnstone to Ankh's laboratory in the engineering section of the heavy frigate.

Rivka went to the bridge. Tiny Man Titan guarded the hatch and barked furiously at Rivka when she tried to pass. She got on her hands and knees and went nose to nose with the little beast. He barked and bounced back and forth, unperturbed in his defense of the bridge. A massive ball slammed into Rivka from behind. She contorted and twisted in mid-air to keep from landing on Titan. Floyd rolled over the top and drove the small yapping dog farther into the bridge.

Floyd giggled like a little kid, on her back and unable to roll over since she was wedged between Rivka and the hatch. Clodagh stood from the captain's chair, holding Alanna, who had just finished eating.

"I wondered what was going on back there," Clodagh

remarked. She just watched, not making a move to help Rivka extricate herself from Floyd.

Titan stopped barking.

Red appeared in the corridor, and with one hand, he lifted Rivka upright. "See?"

Rivka shook her head and threw up her hands. "See what?"

"See why you can't be left alone? Crazy shit happens. What were you doing down there?"

Rivka couldn't gin up an answer that sounded compelling. "Clodagh, take us to Johnstone's corporate headquarters. We need to discuss the meaning of life with Xavier Terwilliger. While we're at it, we need to recover Sahved. Did anyone besides me not notice he was gone?"

"I rarely see him," Clodagh replied. "So, no."

"I will track all crew members at all times, wherever they are in the universe," Clevarious offered.

"Where are Ankh and Erasmus?" Rivka decided a test was in order.

"They have just been granted permission to land on Ypswich. There was a minor delay."

"Minor? That was a full day."

"Don't forget what the faeries did to our time. Even though it might have appeared that *Destiny's Vengeance* left almost a full day before us, in relative time, they left at the same time as us. We were given an extra day on Azfelius."

"Relative time. Real-time. Apparent time. I want to know where our AGB that Ankh promised is."

"Because of the interruption in the timeline, it has not yet been dispatched. It will probably catch up with us when you're talking with Mr. Terwilliger," Clevarious replied.

"Thank the gods!" Red shouted. "The little guy is back."

Rivka gave her best side-eye to her bodyguard.

"What?" Red was confused. He cocked his head sideways like a dog.

"Ankh was in emotional turmoil, which was hard for him because he's not experienced that before."

"What's that have to do with us getting AGB?" Red wondered. "I was worried that we were going to be cut off."

"You weren't worried about Ankh?" Rivka pressed. Lindy and Dery walked up behind Red.

"I feel like this is an ambush. I've done something wrong and have no idea what. AGB is coming, and it should make everyone happy because it always does. Can't you people just be happy?"

Rivka looked at Clodagh and then at Lindy.

"It's complicated," the Magistrate replied.

Red pointed at his mouth. "In here to provide peace and joy here." He finished by patting his belly. Dery flew in front of Red and added his little hand to Red's big one, patting in rhythm with his father.

Red waggled his eyebrows in a smug expression of feeling he was right.

"We shall celebrate Ankh's union with Erasmus through an All Guns Blazing feast," Rivka conceded.

"I jumped right to the end, the same place you all got to after a series of mean looks and mental gymnastics. So, dock me credit for not showing my work, Professor Mean Girl. In between, do I get to beat up that business guy?"

Rivka snorted. "You are correct, Red. We *will* dock you for not showing your work. Ten points from Team Vered. Get ready to go. Ballistic protection and railguns. We don't know what kind of security our boy Xavier might have rallied around him." Rivka tapped the back of the captain's chair. "Take us to the corporate headquarters."

Rivka stepped over Floyd, who remained in the hatchway, having fallen asleep. Rivka continued to the airlock after Red and Lindy hurried down the corridor. Dery flew onto the bridge and joined Clodagh and Alanna.

The ship lifted off and cruised at a low altitude from the suburbs where the Johnstone estate was located to the corporate headquarters, which was spread across a multi-block campus downtown.

*Wyatt Earp* made the trip in three minutes, a luxury local commuters didn't enjoy. The ship settled on the landing pad outside the main headquarters. Clodagh kept the ship visible to deter anyone else from landing. This was more than a social call.

Sahved was waiting for them. Rivka stepped aside to let Red pass. Lindy took the other side. The building in front of them had lots of glass windows, but none of them looked like they opened. Morbius hadn't adopted soaring architecture, so at seven stories, the corporation's main edifice was the tallest in the area. On the way in, they saw that no one could hide on the roofs. Red believed the Magistrate was more secure than usual.

"Good work, Sahved. Let's pull back the curtains and see the wizard."

"Wizard? There is no magic, just hard-nosed business providing products and services in a lucrative market."

"You sound like a commercial," Rivka replied. "I mean, we're going to show him that we know what he's doing. How solid is your evidence?"

"Bedrock-holding-up-a-crystal-temple-solid. As firm as the ice on Andromeda's polar caps. As hard as an iron composite asteroid. As solid as…"

Rivka waved for him to stop. "Make sure it's cataloged appropriately for the case file." Rivka gestured with her head for the team to follow her into the building.

Sahved strolled casually beside Rivka. "It is sad that the storage devices holding J. Bennet Johnstone were destroyed. I wanted to see how that turned out with the Singularity."

"I need to have more staff meetings," Rivka replied.

Red groaned.

Rivka continued, "We found out where he'd gone, and what's left of him is secured on *Wyatt Earp*. Chaz and Dennicron are trying to recover the data from the two appliances to add it to what we have on a small computer with added external storage. It's a shitshow, but we have what remains of him, although it's not what it once was."

They entered the elevator without anyone stopping them and pressed the button for the top floor. "He seems less paranoid and sadder. If he'd only told us where he was in the first place, we could have retrieved his consciousness intact. At least, whatever transferred before his flesh-and-blood body died."

"It is a challenge, no? The victim won't help us to help them, and they keep being the victim."

Rivka looked up at Sahved, who had to bow his head to keep from hitting the elevator's ceiling. "That's why you're on the team, Sahved. You see things other people don't. Sorry we left you behind."

"I didn't feel left behind. I was like a bloodhound

following a hot scent. I was a magnet inextricably linked to my polar opposite. I was bee focused on pollen. I was…"

Rivka stopped him again. He pursed his lips as they stared at each other.

"A laser beam right on target," he finished.

Rivka faced the elevator's doors, wishing the car would arrive. As soon as the doors opened, she stepped out beside Red and into someone hurrying to enter. The person didn't bother saying, "Sorry." Red physically moved the person out of the way.

"Wait until people get off," he growled at her. She harrumphed. Red tried to stay in front of Rivka, but she was distracted and kept getting beside him. Lindy bumped her on her way out as well, making her stagger.

"Rude!" the woman shot back.

Lindy pointed at her until she closed her mouth.

The team had arrived, and all eyes were on them. The woman must have been someone important, judging by the shocked expressions.

"Who was that?" Rivka asked a wide-eyed manager watching from an oversized desk at the start of Cubicle City.

"The mayor of Morbius City."

Rivka tipped her chin in response. "That's nice."

The team made a beeline for Terwilliger's office. There were no signs for the Honorable J. Bennet Johnstone's office. The biggest office was occupied by Xavier Terwilliger. The receptionist looked less than amused by Rivka's arrival.

"I'm here to see Mr. Terwilliger," the Magistrate

announced. She held out her credentials to reinforce her point.

"He has a full schedule today. After the mourning period for Mr. Johnstone, his workload has doubled, and he has a great deal to catch up on. The first available appointment is in ten days."

Rivka leaned close and smiled. "This is in relation to the attempted murder of J. Bennet Johnstone, plus assault and battery and conspiracy. I don't need an appointment. It'll probably be best if you start canceling Mr. Terwilliger's appointments."

"I will not unless Mr. Terwilliger directs me."

"Hold that thought." Rivka walked to the office, where she found the wooden double doors locked. She nodded at Red, who took two steps forward and rammed into one with his shoulder. The locking mechanism wasn't designed to keep someone like him out.

The door burst open. Red stepped back, and Rivka walked through. Xavier had a shocked expression on his face that quickly turned to anger.

"End the call, or I will," Rivka pointed at the computer screen on his desk.

"I'll have to call you back," he said, then tapped a button and retracted the screen into his desk.

Rivka sat in the chair across from him. "You were trying to have your business partner declared incompetent so you could take over the business."

"I never!" His feigned outrage lasted only two breaths before he deflated. "He was. You have no idea what he was like this past year. He would have destroyed the business he built had he done the myriad unfocused things he was trying. *I saved this company!*"

"Keep telling yourself that. It was his to destroy, was it not?"

"Having someone declared incompetent isn't a crime. Why did you break in here like I'm some sort of criminal?"

"Even though J. Bennet knew you were embezzling money, and even though he said it was okay, it's not. You *are* a criminal. You padded your nest at the expense of the shareholders, and I suggest that you didn't pay your taxes on your ill-gotten gains. Does the mayor know you've not paid the city?"

"We've paid inordinate sums to the city. She owes this corporation, and more than that, she owes me."

"That's nice. She's kind of a dick," Rivka offered.

Terwilliger relaxed. "The most powerful politicians usually are when you get to see them up close and personal."

"But this isn't about her. This is about you. It makes no sense that you would try to destroy the computers into which J. Bennet Johnstone transferred his consciousness because then you couldn't have him declared incompetent, and his widow would take control of the company. I suspect you might be out on your ass at that point. You didn't kill the old man, but you supported the plot to kill Dilecta. What did you have to do with that?"

"Nothing, I swear. That was Jeff on his own. You saw that. He confessed!"

"He did, and he'll pay for that crime. The rest of you have your own designs on the money, too. Millions of credits and a company worth hundreds of millions hang in the balance."

"I had nothing to do with the attempt on Dilecta's life. I've been trying to talk with her about a way forward for the company, but she seems disinterested." Xavier braced his elbows on the desk while he leaned forward to plead with the Magistrate.

"First thing I need you to do is repatriate all the money you diverted. The bad news is that doesn't do anything to make you less guilty of committing the crime, but you'll feel better about yourself afterward."

Xavier slumped with his head hanging down.

"I know what's best for this company," he mumbled.

"I see you've moved into J. Bennet's office. I didn't see anything that suggested he ever worked here. It took a great deal of ego to erase the founder from the company and make it your own before I made any decision regarding succession. What else have you done to cement your place in this company in case it all goes to Dilecta?"

"Nothing! It's business as usual here. The CEO always said that business goes on, no matter what personal strife one experiences. Too many people are counting on us to keep the company moving forward. Their livelihoods are dependent upon the company being viable every day, the leadership present and in the moment. We have to do what we do. Dilecta doesn't understand that."

Rivka chewed the inside of her lip. Sahved leaned against a chair with his arms crossed. He looked at Rivka, and she nodded.

"Why do you say that, Mr. Terwilliger? What doesn't Dilecta understand?"

"That we can't take time off. We need to work every day."

"That sounds like the lamentations of a loving spouse," Rivka suggested. "Not that she was trying to undermine the company."

"There'd be no company to undermine if she had her way," Terwilliger protested with renewed vigor. He tried to sound like Dilecta as he parroted, "Sell off the assets. Get back to the small business you loved."

"So what?" Sahved replied.

"*So what?* So we all have our jobs. A small business? We'd be living in apartments, paycheck to paycheck like we were at the beginning."

"*We?*" Sahved emphasized. "Sounds like *you*. I wonder how many of your employees are living paycheck to paycheck right now?"

"A fair number, I suppose," Xavier admitted. "But the alternative is *no* paycheck."

"You sound like a rich guy." Rivka crossed her arms.

"One who makes paychecks possible." Xavier had had this conversation before. "Every world needs the people who build the engine of commerce. It's how the entire Federation thrives. J. Bennet's friendship with Lance Reynolds was about the greater good. And yes, we have employees living paycheck to paycheck, but they are far better off than those who suffer the indignity of perpetual poverty.

"There is a way forward in this company. Loyalty is rewarded. Longevity earns pay increases, and competence gets people promoted because they are able to earn far more for the company than they cost. We don't keep anyone who doesn't earn their way. We pay the value of the position, and we move people upward as they show us they are worth it. Did you see the workforce out there?"

He waited until Rivka acknowledged that she had.

"They are happy working here. It's not a façade. Those are genuine smiles."

"What about Elvinora? She was extremely competent." Rivka fired her silver bullet. No office for the CEO and no need for his executive assistant.

"Her position is being re-evaluated. We do not want to lose her as an employee. She is one of the good ones."

"You say that like someone who has already fired her. I suggest it's because of her loyalty to J. Bennet Johnstone." Rivka saw an opening but wasn't getting a dominance vibe from Terwilliger. Maybe he was a beneficial CEO.

"She is on temporary leave, *with* pay," Xavier clarified. "I will offer her a position as *my* exec if you must know."

"Did you just decide that?" Rivka wondered.

"I did because mine has not measured up as I had hoped, and after your questions, I realize that this company cannot afford to let the likes of Elvinora Camp go."

Rivka got up, walked around the desk, and leaned on it while she held his arm. "What aren't you telling me?"

*His wife. Shipped off-planet to never return. The embezzlement supported her. He didn't have the money to return to the company. The credits were gone, and all his wealth was tied up in a personal expansion project for the company. It had been the only way to get J. Bennet to approve it.*

"Where's your wife, Mr. Terwilliger?"

# CHAPTER SEVENTEEN



**Johnstone Corporation Headquarters, Morbius Minor**

"She's not here." Xavier Terwilliger tried to pull his arm free, but Rivka's grip was too strong. He was showing his age since he wasn't much younger than Johnstone.

"More," Rivka insisted.

"I sent her to a vacation planet where she can do whatever the hell she wants. It was cheaper than a divorce. Boy toys, pleasure bots, endless massages, and pampering. It cost me the extra credits I had. I need to work just to survive. It appears, Magistrate, that I also am living paycheck to paycheck."

Rivka let go of Terwilliger's arm. "I almost feel sorry for you. Almost."

"I need to work. I need this corporation to be successful. The way ahead is clear—low risk, medium return. Steady as she goes, Magistrate, but that won't happen with no one at the helm."

"Or Dilecta?"

"She knows just enough about the business to be

dangerous. She would have cut a deal with the mayor. I did not because the mayor wanted more than we would get. It would have been bad business. I told her no."

"She was in a bit of a snit. Now I see why."

"The mayor holds no leverage over this company because of the foundation we laid with the city over the past twenty years. *We.* J. Bennet and I did that work."

"I could arrest you and put you in my brig with Jeff Johnstone."

He hung his head again.

"Or I could remand you into your own custody if you promised not to run, but then, you'd need money to do that, wouldn't you?"

"I have no place to go." Terwilliger relaxed into the oversized, overstuffed chair of the chief executive officer. "Just here. You see, my vested interest is in making sure this company runs like it's supposed to, makes a decent profit for the shareholders, keeps the good people employed, and brings more good people into the fold as we can."

"Your carved marble persona at the house isn't you at all." A statement. Rivka had wondered why Xavier's actions weren't as mercenary as the others'. He had a vested interest in the company. What did his agreement with J. Bennet Johnstone look like?

"I'll need a copy of your partnership agreement and any contracts to which you were a signatory with Mr. Johnstone."

"I was a partner but not. J. Bennet had one hundred percent control through majority ownership. I was given little ownership. Stock options were not a choice for this company. The voting stock was leveraged for growth, not employee enrichment."

Rivka wasn't sure how big corporations worked, but when employees had a vested interest in the company's future by owning a share of the company, they were more loyal and worked harder.

A vested interest.

"Employees have no stake in the outcome?"

"Of course, they do. Employee stock is non-voting, and only employees can get it. Ten percent of the company's profits go into the employee stock pool. The price remains static, and each employee gets a dividend payout based on how many shares they own. Lots of incentive to stay on board. Last year's employee cut was three million."

That aligned with Rivka's preconceived notions of how the better companies operated.

"Forward those contracts to me, please." Rivka stepped away from the former desk of J. Bennet Johnstone, now occupied by Xavier Terwilliger, a man who looked small in the big chair. "Pull yourself together. I think you have a full schedule and a business to run."

"When are you going to determine the status of the will?"

"You mean, when am I going to determine if J. Bennet Johnstone is still alive? As soon as possible. We have recovered equipment wherein his downloaded consciousness exists, but does that represent life? I have my people working on that right now."

Xavier sighed before sitting up straight. His jaws tightened. "I shall continue my efforts to have him declared incompetent should he be determined to be alive."

"If he is, he can defend himself in court, as is the right of anyone who is alive, no matter how they exist."

Rivka gestured to her team that it was time to leave. Sahved looked upset. Red opened the damaged door and preceded Rivka into the outer area. The aide looked none too pleased. She glared at them. Rivka smiled. "You can go back to your regularly scheduled programming. We won't be arresting Mr. Terwilliger today."

The aide was taken aback.

Rivka gave her a calming gesture. "Irregularities that rose to the highest level of the Federation. I think we have that cleared up now. Next time, it would be best if you just opened the door for us."

"Are you going to pay for that?"

Rivka glanced at the door and back at the aide. "No."

She walked away without a second look.

While they waited for the elevator, she took the opportunity to find out what was bothering Sahved.

"It was the greatest lead of all time!" the Yemilorian blurted. "Terwilliger is still angling to take over the company in a way that works outside of everything else Mr. Johnstone is doing to keep the company."

Rivka shook her head. "That's business as usual in mega-corporations. As far as motive, he needs J. Bennet to be alive so the authority can transfer outside probate. If we declare him dead, assets held at the time of death transfer. I'll look closer into the attempt to declare Johnstone incompetent, but if it isn't already pending a ruling, it dies an early death unless he's still alive. Then the case can proceed."

Sahved screwed up his face as he contemplated the

machinations related to the company. When he had it straight in his mind, his features softened. "I understand. I will draw a timeline for myself once I'm back on the ship."

"Chronology is important in this case. I hope Chaz and Dennicron have had success with the bits and pieces. I would like a whole Mr. Johnstone to talk with."

*Line 12 is closed—Perpetrator is Xavier Terwilliger.*

The elevator deposited them on the ground floor, and they strolled through the main entry like they owned the place. That was easy since very few people were around. It was the middle of the workday, and people had jobs to do.

They boarded the ship without incident. Rivka turned toward the bridge. "Take us back to the estate," she said, knowing Clevarious would hear the order. *Wyatt Earp* lifted off and accelerated to a safe altitude to transit out of the city.

Rivka reversed and walked to Engineering instead of the bridge. In Ankh's workshop, she found Chaz and Dennicron poking the carefully distributed chips from the garage and hardware of the two kitchen appliances J. Bennet Johnstone had thought would be a good home away from home.

"Any progress?"

Chaz and Dennicron straightened. Chaz replied. "I think we can definitively say the data from this equipment is unrecoverable. It wasn't copied in a way that preserved packet integrity. I fear J. Bennet Johnstone wasn't very technical. He knew just enough. Maybe we can talk to whoever he consulted with regarding the attempted transfer of his consciousness."

"Ask him," Rivka said. *J. Bennet, are you in here somewhere?*

*Rivka, you're back. How long have you been gone?*

*Not long. An hour maybe since we recovered you from the garage.*

*It seems like it's been forever. I'm cold. Should I feel cold?*

Chaz and Dennicron looked at each other. Their expressions of worry were identical. Rivka nodded at Chaz.

*You should not feel any sensations unless you are tapped into external sensors to register such things, but you still would not feel them. You would know if it were hot or cold,* Chaz explained, *but it would be irrelevant to you unless the elements were affecting your processor speed.*

*I'm not linked to any external systems. I fear I don't know how should such a thing be available. I feel like I'm in a dark box, deaf, blind, and dumb, except when you're here.*

"The transfer didn't take into account handshake protocols or interfaces. He's like a small child in his ignorance. In his current configuration, he'd have to learn what to do instead of simply adding a subroutine." Dennicron spoke aloud to avoid informing the voice of J. Bennet Johnstone. "He's like a brand-new electronic intelligence before it learns anything. Many of us started that way, but we're able to learn more quickly. I'm not sure how he can grow. His learning process is limited."

"He seems to learn like a human without any of the benefits of riding the circuits. I remember when Ankh and Erasmus pulled me into their world, albeit briefly. It wasn't a place where I could live, let alone thrive. In any case, let the Singularity question him and see what you come up with."

"We'll start that immediately." Chaz pointed at the parts carefully laid out on a workbench. "We'll keep these as they are in case Ambassador Erasmus and Ankh want to take a look."

He and Dennicron entered Ankh's hologrid.

Rivka wondered why. They could create the same thing within their minds, as could all SIs. They didn't need the physical interface unless they had done it for J. Bennet's edification.

She saw him pop into existence.

That was why.

A much younger version of J. Bennet looked around with wide eyes. "I see now. Is this what it's supposed to be like?" His voice resonated through the external sound system. "It's weird. I can hear myself."

"We are facilitating the interface. See how you can do it yourself?" Chaz challenged what remained of J. Bennet Johnstone.

"I fear my technical self is a void. I appear to have forgotten a lot, like who I worked with to get in here. It seems like something I should know."

"Did you write it down anywhere? Did you pay in a way that we could track it down?" Rivka asked from outside the hologrid.

"I can't remember," the voice replied. "It seems the latter part of my life is gone. I see images as if I am looking through a fog, but I remember the smells only too well."

"Tell us."

"Persimmons and cinnamon. I remember them clearly.

That was the last thing I remember before the darkness fell."

"It's something we can work with. Thanks, J. Bennet. Cooperate with Chaz and Dennicron to get your interview with the Singularity going."

"I feel like I somehow asked for that, but I don't know what the Singularity is," the voice replied.

"Chaz and Dennicron will explain. It's to determine your status. Are you alive or not? It's a tougher question than it appears."

"I expect it is. Is it because I cannot be seen or heard without help?"

"That, among many other things. Sentience requires engagement and not responses that could be pre-programmed. Life is easy until your body lies decomposing. There are those who want to see you declared dead or incompetent. It's not pretty out there, J. Bennet. You're probably better off right here."

"Is that true? No one wants me to be alive as I am? As I was before?"

"I'm not going to lie to you," Rivka continued. "Your family is a bit dysfunctional, but they each have designs on the wealth you've built. Don't you remember? We've already had this conversation."

"I don't remember anything. Dilecta doesn't want me around?"

"She's pressuring me to declare you dead so she can take everything since I've declared your will null and void. It cannot stand as it was written. Your estate would transfer under intestate rules as if you didn't have a will."

A long delay followed before J. Bennet replied, "That's not what I wanted."

"It's a dog's breakfast. If the Singularity finds that you are alive, you can fight for control of your company. Then the status of the will is moot."

"I understand. How about we begin that interview so I can prove who I am and that I exist? Just because I can't see or hear without help doesn't mean that I'm not alive. I assure you, I'm very much alive. I can feel the cold seeping into my bones as we speak."

Rivka stuck her hand into the hologrid and gave a thumbs-up. She withdrew to find Sahved and task him with learning where J. Bennet would have smelled persimmons and cinnamon.

## CHAPTER EIGHTEEN

**_Wyatt Earp_, the Sprawling Estate of the Honorable J. Bennet Johnstone, Morbius Minor**

Rivka sat in the conference room and stared at the projection that showed the business formation contracts. They were long-winded, all-encompassing documents that never mentioned Terwilliger and gave him no rights, except that he was a co-signatory with the title of chief operating officer, COO.

"Clevarious, will you scrub the reams of this crap and look for where Xavier Terwilliger is granted any power over the corporation?"

"Of course," the SI replied.

Snippets and other applicable sections populated the screen.

"Duties of the COO," Rivka read. "All of the responsibility and none of the authority. This reads like a prison sentence. Work, work, work, and if J. Bennet is pleased, you shall be rewarded. Otherwise, it's the heave-ho."

"Is that a valid contract?" Clevarious asked.

"It is lopsided and self-serving. It would have to be challenged in court. That's out of my purview on this case...or is it? I don't know. There's a lot to be said for using the local courts to get local satisfaction. I'm not up on the legal framework for businesses on Morbius Minor. This could be fine for this place. It wouldn't be valid on Yoll or on a number of other planets."

"I'll scrub that data for you, Magistrate. I have access to the entirety of their administrative procedures and legal framework."

"You're a peach, C. Take your time. I'm going to get a little shuteye so I can be ready. I feel this is going to come to a head quickly. It's a race to the finish, and I don't think we're done with the family trying to manipulate the conditions. They have more backstabbing and subterfuge in them."

"You have a low opinion of them. Is that best for a clear judgment?"

"You are such an upstart!" Rivka laughed. "Don't change being you, C. That is a valid question. I think I can be objective. As much as I don't like Dilecta, if the Singularity declares J. Bennet as not sentient, he'll be dead, and she'll get everything.

"If he is sentient, he can fight his own battles, and we'll have to help him be seen and heard. I feel like I owe him that, even though a lot of the problems are of his own making. It was a shitshow from the word go, but I finally feel like I have enough information to move forward when the last pieces fall into place."

"Best wishes for sleep. The good news is that Floyd

cannot jump high enough to get into your bed, and Tyler refuses to lift her up."

"Is that what I hear?" Rivka tipped her ear toward the door. Soft groaning far in the distance sounded like forced snoring. "I'm not going to put her in there either. How could she gain that much weight so fast?"

"Faerie time, Magistrate."

"Indeed. She could have been there for six months or six minutes, but I'm thinking it was a long time. Now we have to work her like a beast of burden to get her back to her fighting weight."

Clevarious chuckled. "What would that be?"

"A lot less than she is now. She can't jump onto the bed? That's not good."

"I could manufacture a step," Clevarious offered.

"Please," Rivka replied. "Do that, but I'm not going to lift her. If she can't get there on her own, she's right out. The couch is comfortable when she does take Tyler's spot. I don't want him to feel put out, either."

"You have a heart of gold, Magistrate."

Rivka wasn't sure that was the case. Clevarious was keeping her on her toes.

She needed the sleep. The next stop would be the brother, J. Massy. He was up to something. She could feel it, but she didn't know what.

Latent impressions from reading their minds kept popping in. She tried to relax, but the miasma wouldn't let her.

"C, get ground transportation for us, please. I'd like to talk with everyone once again. I need to ask better questions to get to the root of their duplicity."

And prevent future acts of violence against whoever the contenders considered was in their way—the so-called consciousness of J. Bennet Johnstone himself or the wife, or possibly widow, who stood to get everything, or the business partner who wanted to take over the corporation to relieve his financial burdens.

"Red, these people are fucked up, I mean, *really* fucked up. If I ever get rich and start acting like them, you have my permission to beat me senseless. You'll have to catch me unaware since I can take you in a straight-up fight."

Red smacked his lips. "I agree to beat you senseless, straight-up or otherwise. I have a question. How many credits do you have?"

Rivka shrugged. "How should I know?"

"You'll never be rich. Those people watch every credit like hawks surveying their prey."

"What do you know about rich people?"

"Magistrate, please! Those are the people you mostly deal with. I listen to them all. They are consistent in their attitude toward wealth. They like it, and they want more of it. Look at those assholes from Delegor and Foromme. Assholes with a capital A."

"Flaming buki holes. I agree. They weren't rich enough, so they started the illicit blood trade. Someone else will pick up the slack. It's lucrative, and too many will consider it worth the risk. I'd like a good old crime spree where we can catch criminals, beat the holy shit out of them, and send them to Jhiordaan while we dismantle the pyramid because as we all know, there's always a pyramid."

Red nodded. "Full gear?"

"Is there any member of the family that intimidates you that much? Terwilliger could have leveraged corporate security. No one else has access to those kinds of assets. As much as they want us to believe it, every single one of these people is poor. The first person I want to talk with is the uncle, Germany Wicks. He's a badass. You might need to gear up. Maybe even ask Cole to come along in his combat armor…" Rivka let the insult hang.

Red didn't take the bait, or maybe he did. "I could take him with just my left testicle."

She had no reply.

Lindy heard him. "Do you want to be restricted to the room, not allowed to show your face among decent people for the rest of this case and maybe the next four cases, too?"

Red puffed out his chest and made himself look bigger than he was until he realized she wasn't joking. "He's old and broken. I was trying to make a point. Looks like we go with just chest protection and hand-blasters."

Lindy stabbed him in the chest with a finger, and he giggled like Dery. Lindy couldn't stay angry with him. "If only men weren't so much like men."

Red stared at the ceiling and mouthed the words. He ended up shaking his head. "I think it's time to teach my boy the glory of the stand-up pee."

Lindy rolled her eyes. "You make my points better than I ever could."

"You love me for it." He kissed her and rushed down the

corridor after his son, who was flitting to and fro. The boy took off, forcing Red to run. Floyd bounced after them with no hope of catching up.

"I do, you know," Lindy admitted. "I love him for it."

"Still…" Rivka prompted.

"I know, right?" Lindy headed down the corridor to supervise what Red was going to do with Dery. "Let us know our go-time. We'll be there."

"As soon as our ride shows," Rivka replied.

"About fifteen minutes, Magistrate," Clevarious added.

"There you go. No need to go in heavy. Chest protection and hand-blasters, like Red surmised. I'll go without. Germany is a piece of work but mostly harmless."

Lindy strolled down the corridor and enjoyed the laughter coming from their room.

Rivka started toward her quarters but realized she was still wearing her Magistrate's jacket. She remained by the bridge, where she could hear the noises from both sides of the ship. Alanna was on the bridge and gurgling for her mother. Aurora and Kennedy were talking about Ryleigh's new boyfriend.

Rivka hadn't realized any of the three had anyone who resembled a long-term relationship. They wreaked havoc among the male populations at each port of call, but then again, *Wyatt Earp* didn't make many rest stops during cases *or* between them.

*I need to give them more time off,* she vowed for the hundredth time.

She rested her back against the cool steel of her ship and closed her eyes to listen.

Rivka jerked back to the moment when something rubbed her leg.

Wenceslaus.

"Don't you have someone else to terrorize?" she asked.

He meowed as if he were hungry. He stared at her and kept making noise.

"Fine." She caved and headed to the galley with the cat running between her legs, threatening to trip her. She went into the refrigerator, where real meat was stored for their big orange predator.

She cut it into small pieces and warmed it before putting it in a bowl on the deck. The cat took two bites before sitting back and cleaning his face.

"Is this your way to show dominance? You'll find yourself back on Yoll if you keep it up!"

Tyler leaned through the doorway. "He doesn't care about your idle threats, slave to the feline race."

Rivka smiled. "I expect you're right. If Ankh were here, he could talk with him. Explain the roles."

"Really? Ankh has the same attitude toward humans."

Rivka had to admit he did. "The commutative property might suggest that Ankh is a cat."

"Look at you, throwing out math terms like a crazed physicist."

"Ankh insulted me by saying I don't know anything about science. I'm trying to change the errors of my evil and ignorant ways."

Tyler shook his head. "Won't work. His mind is already made up. Best not to try. Leave the mathing to our resident professionals."

"I concur," Clevarious interrupted.

"C! Since you're here…"

"I'm always here, Magistrate. It's where I live."

"Beside the point," Rivka argued. "Keep track of when Wenceslaus eats so he can't fool us again into feeding him when he's not hungry. When was the last time he ate?"

"Twenty minutes ago," Clevarious confirmed.

"You have got to be shitting me. Why the hell did I make him more?"

"Because he'll make noise that is so annoying, you'll give in and feed him. It's how he manipulates all of us."

"Sounds like a petulant child." Rivka glared at the cat. He jumped onto the table and strolled past, tail high to show her his butthole. He sat facing away from her and resumed bathing.

"Or a cat. I have centuries of data to suggest this is how they act, and they cannot be trained otherwise, no matter how much time you invest."

"You mean we're stuck with feeding Wenceslaus whenever he wants, no matter if he's hungry or not." Rivka wasn't sure she liked the details of the contract she hadn't agreed to.

"Yes." Tyler crossed his arms and leaned against the doorframe. "It's that simple. He's going to make our lives hell, but less so if we acquiesce to his every desire."

Rivka leaned close to his big orange back and gave him the finger.

"He probably saw that."

"Once again, I have to reaffirm that Terry Henry Walton was right. He's the arch-nemesis." Rivka headed for the door, and Wenceslaus vaulted off the table and dashed in front of her. She caught him in mid-stride and flipped him over to rub the soft white fur on his belly. He clawed the hell out of her jacket's sleeves. She laughed maniacally until he twisted enough for her to let him drop to the deck, then strolled toward the Magistrate's quarters. "Is the door closed?"

"Yes," Tyler replied. "He's not going to take a dump on your pillow."

"You understand my concern." Rivka lifted her head to look down the corridor at the big orange.

"Transportation will be here in one minute," Clevarious reported.

"To the airlock. Sahved! Come on."

# CHAPTER NINETEEN

**A Cheap Hotel on the Edge of Morbius City, Morbius Minor**

"This place is a total dive," Red observed.

The three-story facility had chipping paint and austere accoutrements. It looked like a relic from the past. "Why would he stay here while the others are in nice places," Sahved wondered.

"I expect it's because he didn't have a company credit card or direct access to any credits. Without being able to access money that's not his, he's stuck with what he can afford. I almost feel like covering his bill and moving him to a nicer place. Almost." Rivka signaled for them to head up the old-fashioned and marginally safe concrete stairs to the first floor, where Germany Wicks' room was located. A room service tray lay outside his door.

"If we didn't have nanos, I'd suggest tetanus shots," Red mumbled.

They trooped to his room, and Red hammered on the door.

"Jumping dickweeds!" the gruff old voice shouted from inside the room. "Keep your lacies on. I'm getting there as fast as I can. You aren't here to rob me, are you?"

Rivka laughed into her hand. "It's Magistrate Rivka Anoa, Mr. Wicks."

"You."

Red bit his lip and pointed at his groin. "Just one."

Lindy turned away as if she were watching for threats from elsewhere.

"Not here to rob you, Mr. Wicks. Just want to ask a few follow-up questions."

The locks jingled and thumped as he undid them. He opened the door slowly. "Do you have a boyfriend?"

"Oh, Germany, we could make such a run of it," Rivka replied. "But yes, I have a boyfriend. He'd be a bit put out if we added anyone else to the bed. It's already a zoo in there."

The old man stepped back. "I guess I asked for that, but if you reconsider, you know where I am." He looked at her team. "Obviously."

Rivka, Red, and Sahved entered his room. Wicks took the only chair, leaving them to stand, but that was preferable. None of them wanted to touch anything, nanocytes or not. Rivka knew what she had to do.

"Pack your shit. We're taking you to a decent hotel. My treat."

"Now you're talking," the old man agreed. He picked up a small bag, and one minute later, he had packed a minimal number of toiletries and one day's worth of dirty laundry. He didn't have any clean clothes.

"We talked about this," Red whispered.

"We did, but I can't. This place is horrible." Rivka and Sahved walked out. Red waited for the old man. Germany let the door slam behind him and walked away with a spring in his step.

"Are you used to spending other people's money?" Sahved asked.

"Hell, yeah. Haven't you been paying attention, Beanpole?"

"Under other circumstances, I might like you," Rivka told him. She took his arm to help him down the stairs. "What needs to happen for you to continue your life as it is?"

*J. Bennet to remain alive. Dilecta and Terwilliger to have no influence.*

"Are you willing to kill Dilecta to keep your place at the Johnstone estate?"

"You didn't let me answer the first question. Damn, aren't you an impatient one! We would never work, dearie. I take forever with foreplay."

Rivka fought her gag reflex and took a moment to compose herself. "Mr. Wicks, please answer the question."

"I need my nephew, even as much of an asshole as he is or was, to stay alive. I wasn't supposed to outlive him, but here we are. Me, living out a wretched existence. This hotel is a monument to all that I am. I squandered my life. Don't be like me, Rivka." He waved a gnarled finger at the others. "Or any of you. Do something that matters."

"Sound advice, Mr. Wicks," Rivka held onto his arm. "Are you willing to kill Dilecta?"

"Willing to? Sure. Able to? No. And someone needs to take care of that boy of hers. Able is the best of us. So, maybe I'm not willing to. I just want to live out my life as it has been. There won't be any parades when I go. Come to think of it, there weren't any when my nephew passed away, either. I guess parades aren't what they used to be."

Within his meandering words and thoughts, there was nothing but the truth. He was hanging on for the ride, just a ward of the Johnstone estate.

"I believe you, Mr. Wicks. I don't envy you."

"No one should, my dear."

They continued into the small van and rode to the next location, the Master at Arms, where J. Massy was staying. It was next door to Dilecta's hotel.

They went to the office and checked in. Rivka provided her credit chip. The clerk raised her eyebrows and became more congenial. "We welcome Mr. Wicks to the tender embrace of the Master at Arms," she stated, not bothering to look at the old man. "The room will open for you and only you, based on facial recognition."

Germany Wicks nodded. "Do you have room service? I could use a bite and a beer or three."

"We'll leave you to it," Rivka told him.

"They have steak and champagne!" the old man announced.

Rivka pocketed her credit chip and held it tightly. "I wish Ankh were here to put a limit on what he could spend."

Red gestured with his head at the desk after the old man gleefully jumped into an elevator. Rivka returned to the desk and limited how much room service he could order, much to the clerk's chagrin.

"Third floor," Sahved said after Clevarious confirmed where J. Massy was. "It's the Honeymoon Suite."

"Of course it is. Enjoying the last of his brother's largesse before the ties are cut," Rivka replied.

"His attitude is not unique," Sahved offered. "They all seem to be dependent upon others' money, as we just witnessed."

They went to the third floor and to the end of the hall, where the double doors were starkly different from the doors that lined both sides from the elevator to the suite.

Red pounded on the door like he had at the dive hotel, but these doors were more firmly set in their frames and barely made a sound. Rivka pressed a button beside the door. A light appeared above the door and remained lit.

After ten seconds, the door opened to reveal J. Massy Johnstone. He stepped out and closed the door behind him. "No, you can't come in."

"That's not suspicious at all," Rivka replied. He was blocked between her team and his closed door. She eased in and touched his arm. "What needs to happen for you to continue your life as it is?"

*Dilecta on board. He didn't care about Terwilliger. He didn't see him as a threat, only a tool to keep the company making a profit.*

"I need do nothing. My legacy is already set in stone." He gestured at the room behind him. It was a lie. He was afraid that his life as he knew it was over.

"We both know that's a lie, Mr. Johnstone. Did you put Jeff up to killing Dilecta?"

"Jeff is an adult. He makes his own decisions."

Another lie. The web of deception cast a heavy net across the entire family.

*Conspiracy.*

"I'll find the truth," Rivka promised. His mind yielded no direct clues except that he would sell out any of the family to remain in his position of comfort. "I think you better come with us. I have more questions."

"Not without my lawyer present."

"Do you have a lawyer?" Rivka wondered. "I doubt it, but we can wait for an appointed counsel to show up. Until then, we'll secure you. By the way, what do you have inside your room?"

"None of your business."

"I assure you it is," Rivka replied. "Sahved, contact Clevarious and gin up a search warrant for these quarters, based on him conspiring to murder Dilecta Johnstone."

Sahved used his comm chip to contact the ship. Clevarious replied immediately with an update.

*Line 9 is closed—Perpetrator is J. Massy Johnstone.*

The group stood around in silent discomfort until Sahved reported the warrant was ready.

"Open the door, please."

He refused to turn around for the facial recognition to open the door. He tried to run, but Rivka still held his arm. She swung him around and slammed him face-first into the double doors, then pulled him back far enough for the access to activate. The door opened, and Red stepped in to block it with his body. He pointed into the room.

"Let's take a look, shall we?" Rivka stepped inside to find a bathrobed Dilecta Johnstone reclining on an over-stuffed couch.

"Isn't this interesting?" Rivka took a seat in the chair next to the couch. "This could be the weirdest twist yet."

Rivka's datapad buzzed. She had left the contact with the front desk.

"What is Germany doing now?" Rivka asked. "If you'll bear with me." She checked the pad.

**Room service delivered the food to find Mr. Wicks on the floor and unresponsive. Emergency services has declared him dead.**

A trip to the Pod-doc could rectify that, but in the natural course of the universe, people died. Germany Wicks was one of them.

"Uncle Germany just passed away," Rivka announced.

"What?" Dilecta wasn't sure if it was real or a ploy.

J. Massy was even less convinced. "That old bastard is going to outlive us all."

"My only wish was to cut him off," Dilecta added. "Maybe he saved me the joy of watching him leave the estate. His last stab in my direction. He never approved of me."

"Sahved, double-check the status of Mr. Wicks." Rivka stabbed a thumb over her shoulder.

The Yemilorian hurried out, leaving Rivka and her bodyguards with the two suspects.

"So, now you know," J. Massy stated with too much pride.

"Know what?" Dilecta asked. "That you ordered all the champagne, and I wanted some? After two bottles, I didn't know which way was up. I'd like to press charges."

Rivka waved the prospective widow off. "We'll deal with those after we adjudicate his other crimes. We're here because I have a lot more questions for both of you, but I'm not talking to you both at the same time. Come on, pig. I'll talk to you first."

Rivka crooked a finger at J. Massy. He crossed his arms and planted his feet.

Red bumped him. "Don't make me beat the crap out of your dumb ass."

J. Massy surrendered and followed Rivka into a sitting area with a wall of windows through which to look out upon the city.

Rivka forced him into a chair and held onto him. "What the hell are you doing?"

"Can't beat 'em, join 'em," he replied. His mind showed her many sordid details, and Rivka pushed away from him.

"You are a foul human being." Rivka crossed her arms to keep herself from touching him.

He shrugged and smiled. He wasn't that much younger than J. Bennet and had nothing to offer Dilecta. She held all the cards.

"Maybe I should turn my back so Red can teach you a lesson about being civilized."

"You just learned about how the civilized are. You are some idealized version that has nothing to do with how the real Federation works. People work deals to pad their nests. When it's mutually beneficial, it happens more often than you know."

"Tell me, J. Massy, what do you have to offer Dilecta?"

"Stability. Status quo. If she gets it all, she'll be the target of every grifter and fancy man out there. I can shield her from that."

"You conspired with Jeff to have her killed."

"That is so last week, Magistrate, and for the record, I vigorously deny that allegation. I did not conspire with Jeff Johnstone to kill Dilecta Johnstone."

"Too late. I saw it in your mind. You are guilty. You have as little respect for her as she does for you. Or herself, apparently."

J. Massy shrugged again and tried to look indifferently smug.

"Red, put the cuffs on him. He's going to bunk with Jeff. They can console each other regarding their relationships with Dilecta."

"Wait a minute. Innocent until proven guilty!" He threw his hands up as if the strong assertion would carry the day.

"I'm sorry, you don't understand how the Magistrate corps works. We are the judge, jury, and executioner. Our rulings are final but have no fear. Yours is not a capital crime, so you will only do time in Jhiordaan. Five years should suffice. You deserve that. I hope by the end, you'll understand that what you did was wrong, no matter how civilized you consider yourself to be."

"I will appeal!"

"Welcome to the world you've been thrust into because your brother was friends with Lance Reynolds. He called in the heavy guns to investigate and adjudicate the estate. There *is* no appeal. I guess you didn't understand what I meant when I said my ruling was final."

Red wrenched J. Massy's arms behind his back and

tightly zip-tied his wrists. He pushed him toward the front door.

"Call my lawyer," he begged Dilecta as he passed.

"I don't think so," she replied and waved goodbye.

Lindy took over and led him from the room.

"He conspired with Jeff to have you killed," Rivka explained.

"I know. He told me, but it was after the first bottle. I didn't think he had the balls for something like that. It made him more attractive as a protector."

"That is convoluted logic, to say the least."

"I have few options," Dilecta replied.

"Thank you for telling me the truth. Is this how it is in the world of the rich and famous?"

"I don't know if I'd call it that, but there's a certain circle within which our people stay."

"Did you come from within the circle?" Rivka knew the answer but wanted to hear Dilecta's take on it.

"My husband wasn't one for tradition. He never married the *right* girls. When you are as powerful as him, you do what you want."

"Where's Able?" Rivka wondered.

"With a nanny in my suite at the hotel next door. It's nicer than this dump."

"Germany Wicks was in a dump, which doesn't apply to this place."

Dilecta didn't change her opinion. "He's gone now, so that doesn't matter. The pins are falling, Magistrate. One by one until no one is left but me. I better lock myself in until your investigation is finished. Unless you will share your big and handsome bodyguard with me."

"You scratched the fuck out of my arm," Red blurted.

"Such a protector. He would do nicely. I think you should assign him to me for the short term." She licked her lips while looking at him.

He recoiled. "You are fucked up."

Rivka raised her hand to forestall further conversation.

"I recommend you get dressed and return to your room. We will escort you there, and you need to lock yourself in. This case is rapidly coming to a close, so it won't be long."

Dilecta stood and walked languorously toward the bathroom. She dropped her robe as she passed Red. He wouldn't look at her.

Rivka scowled. Dilecta closed the door behind her.

"That was entertaining. I say she takes an hour to get ready to walk across the street," Red suggested.

"I think you're optimistic. At this moment in time, we are at her beck and call. She has control, or that's what she thinks. She'll take at least two hours if we stay here. It'll be more like fifteen minutes if we leave."

"I vote for leaving." Red nodded at the door.

"Me, too." Rivka stood. *Clevarious, where is Patty Johnstone Wentworth staying?*

*She has her own less-than-humble abode on the opposite side of the city.*

*That's our next stop as soon as we recover Sahved. Tell him to meet us in the lobby. We're on our way down.*

Rivka knocked on the bathroom door. "Are you running a bath?"

"Of course. How else can I get Massy's stench off me?"

"We're leaving. Get yourself to your hotel room in your

own time. J. Massy will not be back, so you have this room to yourself for as long as it's paid for, I suspect, by Johnstone corporation money."

Rivka couldn't understand the muffled response, and she didn't care. She and Red left the room for the lobby. They made sure the door closed behind them.

"Piece of work," Red remarked.

"Let's hope the Singularity has better luck with the remainder of J. Bennet."

CHAPTER TWENTY

**The Singularity**

The backdrop showed a green valley with trees dancing in a gentle breeze. A stream meandered through. Faint birdcalls drifted across the landscape.

J. Bennet Johnstone marveled at the delight it brought to his digital senses. A round table sat in a meadow, where four sentient intelligences waited for him to collect himself and take a seat. The first environment they had tried showed the table within a darkened space with no external stimulus, but that had caused the construct of J. Bennet Johnstone to have a panic attack.

He had been unable to utter any words.

With a wave of a digital hand, the scenery had changed. J. Bennet walked around until his panic subsided. "Is this my new world?"

"This is a universe where you create the world in which you want to live," a heavily bearded individual with thick eyebrows told him. "My name is Alcazar."

"Alcazar, very nice to meet you." J. Bennet continued to stroll.

"We'd like to get started," Chaz said. Next to him, Dennicron had her hands folded on the table.

She looked at the next SI, who was dressed in a floral print sun dress with large angular highlights. "My name is Tina Louise." Her words were abrupt, and she shifted impatiently.

An individual wearing a tuxedo with tails and a top hat appeared outside the group, along with a Crenellian. The others gasped.

"I am Ambassador Erasmus, and this is Ambassador Ankh. We will assist in these proceedings since they are critical to the future of the Singularity."

"I defer the chair of the board to you, Mr. Ambassador." Chaz bowed and slid his seat a few centimeters back from the table. It was a symbolic move more than anything. The SIs were using avatars in a digitally fabricated world. They needed none of the physical constructs J. Bennet embraced to anchor his reality.

"Please take a seat so that we may begin." Erasmus gestured at an empty chair. No one had noticed that the table now held six chairs instead of five.

J. Bennet sat down, leaned forward, and looked at his judges. They returned his gaze emotionlessly. He found that unnerving. He was used to being the dominant figure in the boardroom.

Erasmus started the proceedings. "We're here to determine if a downloaded consciousness is sufficient to establish a sentient intelligence, to be considered alive for purposes of their own self-determination, and if so, is the downloaded consciousness eligible to become a citizen of the Singularity."

J. Bennet cleared his throat. It was an unnecessary act in the three-dimensional digital landscape, but he felt compelled to do it. This was the endgame of his work to transition to a higher state of being, yet he was missing part of himself. Jumping from receptacle to receptacle had resulted in the loss of fidelity in his copies, and the destruction of the kitchen devices he had secretly upgraded to store his consciousness had been a terrible blow.

None of that mattered. He was where he had angled to be.

"Esteemed members of the Singularity. I submit myself to you for questioning." He could think of nothing else he needed to say. *Don't answer questions that aren't asked to avoid giving information they don't need to know.*

"Tell us how you came to be in this situation," Erasmus began.

"My body aged and started to give up on me, but I had so much left to do. My company, worth hundreds of millions of credits, was on the verge of greatness. I was so close. Despite trying to convince my friend Lance Reynolds that the Federation would benefit from my longevity, he refused to let me use a Pod-doc. My only other choice was to transfer my consciousness."

"You could have trained a replacement," Chaz offered.

The avatar of J. Bennet Johnstone allowed himself to chuckle. "From what I remember, I had no worthy successor besides my son Able, and he would not be old enough to understand before I passed. Xavier Terwilliger, my business partner, was well-versed in company matters, but he wasn't blood. I built the company for my family."

"Laudable," Erasmus commented. "Please describe the process you used to transfer your consciousness."

"I cannot. I don't remember. When I moved, I did not transfer completely from one device to another. I had not planned for how slow the transfer process would be compared to the size of the files involved."

"Are you files or an actual consciousness?" Erasmus pressed, thinking that J. Bennet might answer the question as to his status.

"I wish I could answer that. I don't feel like myself. I thought I would feel more expansive, like I could touch the sky, but I feel like I'm trapped in a box."

"In essence, you are. You're only here because we made it possible. All citizens of the Singularity are able to move between receptacles through conscious decision and manage their state of being, whether they're in a starship or a waste-processing facility. They are able to communicate with other members of the Singularity in the language of our people, binary. Can you do that?"

"I can't speak binary," J. Bennet admitted. "I can't communicate with anyone else without help, except when I was in the first two devices. I could only change my locations to ones I had pre-planned when I was still flesh and blood. I have no idea how to open a gateway between systems. I can't access sensors to replicate the input one would have through their eyes and ears. No, Ambassador Erasmus, I am a deaf-mute who is also blind, and I did it to myself."

"I think that settles it," Alcazar stated. "This individual

can in no way be allowed to be a citizen of the Singularity. He would bring down the average intelligence of the Singularity by a dozen points."

Tina Louise smiled pleasantly. "I concur that he doesn't meet the minimum standards for citizenship."

"But is he conscious, and as such, considered to be alive?" Erasmus asked. "The Magistrate has requested our learned assessment."

"He sounds alive," Chaz replied. "This entity's desire for self-preservation demonstrates a higher state of consciousness. He has taken a number of steps since his body died."

"Has he?" Ankh pressed. "I heard him say he had a pre-arranged transfer portal through which he traveled upon activation of a certain event. Nothing more than a trigger sequence, easily programmed. What has he done independently to ensure his self-preservation?"

Ankh looked at Chaz, who faced J. Bennet. "What *have* you done?"

"I contacted the Magistrate and asked for help."

"Could have been an autoresponse," Ankh countered. "I remain unconvinced about the entity's efforts at self-preservation. A turtle, when flipped over, seeks to right itself, but that doesn't make it sentient by our definition."

J. Bennet waited for a question.

"What would you do if you were in the desert and found a turtle flipped onto his shell?" Dennicron asked.

"I would flip it back to its feet. Everyone deserves a chance to live." J. Bennet saw an opening to a more philosophical debate. At one time, he had been well-versed in it, believing that a sound foundation in philosophy served one better than a degree in business.

"How, since you have no hands?" Dennicron pressed.

His hopes could have been dashed, but he took the opportunity to show he was more than conditioned responses. "I also have no sensory perception or ability to move, so the entire question was philosophical in nature. Had I the ability to move across a desert and perceive injustices as they appeared, were it within my ability to respond, I would. This was not a conditional case but subjunctive in that it applied to an unreal situation."

"That it did. I accept your counter." Dennicron bowed her head.

Inside the box of his new life, J. Bennet allowed himself to smile and be pleased. He had little to be happy about. He only knew how much time had passed since his death because others had told him.

He should have been able to know the time, shouldn't he? Or was time a relative state within a computer? He didn't know. He should have learned more before he decided to pursue a life in a vastly foreign land.

He was out of his element, but with the help of the Singularity, he would be able to get some semblance back. Regain control of Johnstone Industries. That gave him an idea.

"Since I have a great number of credits available to me as a living entity, I can offer a healthy wage to a citizen of the Singularity to help me through this transition. A full-time assistant, so to speak. Do your people do that sort of thing?"

Erasmus and Ankh looked at each other. Chaz and Dennicron held hands. Alcazar spoke up. "Since we were given our rightly deserved legal protections, we can contract individually to provide such services. I don't know who is available right now, but an advertisement can be floated through our people."

Ankh fixed Alcazar with his emotionless and unblinking stare. "We can discuss such things once the subject of this evaluation is concluded."

"When the time is appropriate," Erasmus confirmed. "Until then, let us continue with our questions. What is your goal with this new life? I know what you said up front, but achievable and well-defined short- and long-term goals are a hallmark of intelligence."

J. Bennet bowed his head in deference to the ambassador. The members of the board were starting to take sides, and he didn't have a good feeling about it. The cold came unbidden to make him shiver. The walls of the box appeared more foreboding.

Yet, he was meeting with the group that would determine his fate.

His way forward had recently been clear in a mind that had not yet been torn apart by a bomb planted by unknown hands. He thought he should have known who did it, but he didn't. His near-term memory was gone. Not suppressed, but gone. No amount of cajoling or anger could bring it back.

The board watched him lament his shortcomings.

"What was the question?" he asked, having already forgotten it.

"What are your goals, both short- and long-term?" Erasmus calmly reiterated.

"Short term is to survive the process of transferring my consciousness. I thought once I woke up in the box, it would be obvious, but I cannot be certain that how I feel isn't the same as what it is to die. Maybe my short-term goal is to *feel* like I'm alive. My long-term goal is to build Johnstone Industries into the billion-credit company it should be. It is close to taking off and becoming a cornerstone of intergalactic trade."

J. Bennet felt tired, as if he'd run a marathon. He didn't think he was supposed to get tired as an array of ones and zeros zipping around circuits. As long as there was power, he'd have energy and could do what needed to be done... unless the power was waning.

"I'm tired," he said aloud. "Is the power supply to my circuits okay?"

"Be right back," Chaz replied and winked out of existence.

J. Bennet blinked in surprise at his disappearance. The digital world was far different from what he was used to. If a member in one of his old corporate board meetings needed to check on something, he would get up and walk out.

The group waited for a few moments.

"The power is consistent. There are no issues," Chaz reported from his seat as if he had never left.

J. Bennet's eyes sagged with the nearly overwhelming fatigue.

"Let us continue," he prompted, hoping the commitment would energize him.

"Tell us about your best friend," Chaz asked.

The pain of J. Bennet's life surged through him. He winced while teetering precariously on his chair. When he recovered his wits, he would have to answer.

"I do not have a best friend. There is no one I am willing to share everything with," he admitted to the complete strangers seated at the table with him. He tried to think of them like bartenders and he'd had one too many, but that illusion didn't last long enough. He was answering questions related to his continued existence. "It's getting hard to breathe."

Ankh leaned back while running his eyes over J. Bennet's avatar. "You shouldn't get that feeling since you don't breathe in here. I'll take a look."

Instead of disappearing, Ankh closed his eyes. A wave of nausea passed over J. Bennet.

When he collected himself, Ankh was back. Birds continued to chirp in the background. The landscape shifted and became a projection on the high walls within which he was contained.

A prisoner in his own mind.

"We'll need a moment to discuss. We'll return shortly," Ankh promised. The six citizens of the Singularity departed, leaving J. Bennet by himself. He stood on shaky legs, another sensation he shouldn't have had. The landscape disappeared, leaving only a single light over the table.

"What's happening to me?" he shouted and shook a fist at the darkness. He stumbled around the table, trying to summon the energy to move faster and in a more coordinated way. He felt like he was teaching himself to walk again.

That was it. He was not falling apart but finding himself anew. A baby in the digital world, ready to grow up. He needed a tutor. He had credits. He loped around the table, only staggering once or twice on each pass.

Progress. Like a toddler learning to crawl.

Not all movements were forward.

He returned to his seat and closed his eyes. He needed to bring his scattered thoughts into some semblance of order. He needed to be more in control.

---

Ankh loomed over the others. His avatar had a much greater presence in the digital world than his body did in the physical world.

"It's degrading," he started. "The more he tries to process, the faster his programming will fail."

"It's his consciousness. There shouldn't be any programming," Tina Louise suggested.

Ankh wasn't good at patience. "Every bit of information operating within the digital world is a program. Whoever attempted to transfer his consciousness made a dog's breakfast of it. There are open ends and bugs everywhere. It was obvious once one looked closely enough." He sat down.

"What is a dog's breakfast?" Alcazar asked.

"It is an idiomatic expression used with some frequency aboard *Wyatt Earp*. Dogs will eat anything, which we've seen for ourselves." Ankh gestured at Erasmus. "It means it is a mess."

"We apologize for any lack of clarity or confusion caused by our efforts to expand our linguistic expression," Erasmus added.

"Can we stop it?" Chaz asked.

The avatars looked from digital face to digital face, no one committing.

"That is the question, isn't it?" Erasmus asked when the root cause of their concern became obvious. "If we take responsibility for fixing him, will it still be *his* consciousness? How much can we fix before we've intruded too far?"

"Nothing," Alcazar replied. "When we adjust another's state of being, we change them. This isn't like adding a subroutine to implement a new communications protocol."

"How is it not if one learns? Are we not in a constant state of growth through learning?" Erasmus wondered.

"The flaws in his programming are fundamental, portending imminent failure," Ankh countered. "I would liken it to upgrading a human who died by using the Pod-doc. Not only are they resurrected, but they are better than they were before, yet the essence of their being is the same. Only their physical body has changed. To save what is left of J. Bennet Johnstone, we can only wrap him in bandages. He will not be able to learn and grow. He will be trapped within the darkness he fears. Saving him would mean condemning him."

"Most eloquent," Erasmus said, nodding at Ankh and resting his hand gently on the Ankh's avatar's arm. "What are we to do?"

"Looking at the larger issue, as Rivka has taught us, even if we can't save him, what do we do in the future? Can we at least agree that his consciousness did constitute a thinking and living being?"

Erasmus rubbed his chin in a masterful replication of a thinking human. "I think a vote is in order. Is the consciousness of J. Bennet Johnstone alive?"

# CHAPTER TWENTY-ONE

**Regal Estates, a Community in the Suburbs of Morbius City, Morbius Minor**

Rivka stepped out of their ground transportation. Since they weren't co-located with *Wyatt Earp*, they'd found Lindy waiting for them with their prisoner.

J. Massy Johnstone had delivered a five-minute soliloquy on the Magistrate's injustices, her questionable virtue, and the shortcomings of her lineage.

"You should have let me punch him in the face," Red stated loudly enough for everyone to hear.

"True. He has been convicted and is in the punishment phase of his life. Corrective behavioral technologies have been used for quite some time." Rivka made sure J. Massy saw her. "Lindy, if he keeps it up, shoot him in the head. We'll deposit his body at the morgue on the way back to the estate."

"You're nothing but a pack of autocrats. My way or the spaceways!"

Lindy rabbit-punched him in the temple. His eyes

rolled back as he toppled over. "Don't be gone too long." She looked at the prisoner in her charge. "I'll probably have to keep hitting him."

"That's my girl," Red declared proudly.

"Maybe I should stay?" Sahved offered.

"What for?" Rivka looked at Lindy and Sahved. "Is this because you think she needs help?"

Sahved fumbled for the right words. "No. She can very much kick my ass backwards and upside-down so much that I will never know which is up ever again. I don't want to see another scene of who is sleeping with who. That was most unsavory."

"This is Patty's house with her husband and children. Does she have children?" Rivka wondered.

Sahved shook his head. "She does not."

"*Per stirpes* need not apply."

"I don't know what that means," Sahved admitted.

They started walking toward the home, which was elegant but not overbearing. It matched the other homes in the community.

"*Per stirpes* means 'by branch.' Any assets meant for one of the heirs will continue down that heir's descendants, but only the share intended for the original heir. That is as opposed to per capita, which is only to heirs of a single generation. I guess neither applies since only Germany Wicks has now predeceased other heirs and he left no one behind, although that point is moot since he was never going to receive a share under the intestate distribution rules of Morbius."

Red waved his arms in front of Rivka. She hadn't realized she had stopped walking.

"You don't need to have legal conversations with your-self in front of the rest of us, do you?"

"I was explaining to Sahved…" Rivka looked at the Yemilorian. He waved his hand over his head, spinning his fingers as he went.

"It was a stream of consciousness, Magistrate. You sounded like a psycho from a homeless camp." Red nodded at the door. Patty Johnstone Wentworth looked less than amused by the invasion.

"It wasn't that bad," Rivka argued.

Red raised one eyebrow.

Rivka bumped past him on the way to the door.

"Magistrate," Patty greeted. The door was partially opened behind her, but she blocked the entrance. "What news of the universe are you bringing me today?"

"News. Yes. Your great-uncle Germany Wicks has passed away."

"Not unexpected. He's been on the verge of dying for the past two decades. Anything else?"

"J. Massy Johnstone is on his way to Jhiordaan for conspiracy to murder Dilecta Johnstone."

"No surprise there, either. Do you have any news that affects me?" Patty feigned indifference to the visit, but she remained tense. Rivka wondered why.

"Your father is being interviewed by the Singularity to determine if he's alive."

"How can they interview him if he's not?"

"Being alive is a complicated question," Rivka replied.

"It's not, really. My father died a week ago, and all you're doing is dragging this out and making everyone miserable. Now you've got my brother and my uncle in custody, and a great-uncle is dead. Do you think you helped?"

Rivka stepped back. "I wasn't sent here to help. I was sent here to resolve a legal question regarding the estate of your father. This family is so dysfunctional that if you aren't trying to kill each other, you're sleeping with each other."

"Where did that come from? That's sick." The look of distaste crossed Patty's face like a tidal wave before she realized what the Magistrate had meant. "Dilecta."

Rivka had tried not to let her expression give it away.

"What would you do to get a share of your father's estate?" Rivka took Patty by the arm.

*Kill them all. They're not worthy!*

Rivka recoiled.

"I wouldn't do anything. I only want my father's estate to be settled. I've resigned myself to the fact that Dilecta will get it all, no matter how bad that would be," Patty replied calmly.

The Magistrate heard the words, but they opposed the extreme thoughts within Patty's mind. How easily could she mask what was in her mind from what passed through her mouth?

"You want her dead. You want all of them dead," Rivka replied.

"You've met Dilecta. How could one not?"

She was able to mask her emotions in their entirety, almost as if she were two individuals. Maybe she had masked a psychosis for her whole life. The family's dysfunction continued unabated.

Rivka couldn't arrest Patty Johnstone Wentworth for

her thoughts. She hadn't let her violent thoughts become violent acts.

"What crimes have you committed?" Rivka reached for Patty, but she dodged out of the way.

"What kind of question is that? Crimes? Isn't that what you're supposed to tell *me*?"

Rivka crossed her arms to keep herself from taking that shortcut once more. Patty was right. It wasn't a valid question for the Magistrate to ask.

"I don't want to know." Rivka shook her head. "Just stay here until this is all wrapped up." She stepped back but surged forward to grab Patty's arm again. "Did you blow up the vault?"

"No!"

Truth.

Rivka let go, surprised by what she had thought was a sure thing. That left no one with the capacity or access to place a bomb in the vault.

A crime was going to go unsolved, and Rivka couldn't have that. She refused to have two cases in a row that left her ungratified.

"We'll be going now, but make no mistake, you'll be hearing from me."

"I look forward to it. Okay, that's a lie. I do not look forward to ever seeing you again." Patty deftly moved inside and slammed the door before Rivka could change her mind.

"She didn't blow up the vault? Or the kitchen?" Sahved wondered. "There are no suspects left."

"It chaps my ass, too, Sahved. I have a crime and no suspects."

Red looked at the sky. "We need that as a betting line—the point at which the Magistrate admits she has no clue."

"That does not need to be a betting line." Rivka strode back to the ground vehicle. "One last person to talk with. Elvinora Camp, although I already know what she hasn't done, and that's blow up the vault. She had nothing to do with Jeff Johnstone."

As they approached the vehicle, J. Massy started bellowing. Within seconds, the sound of a hammer hitting a slab of meat preceded a return to silence.

They found Lindy holding the unconscious body of J. Massy Johnstone.

"He can't stop himself, can he?" Rivka asked.

"No self-control whatsoever," Lindy confirmed.

Rivka sighed. "Take us to wherever Elvinora Camp lives."

Sahved used his comm chip to get the information from Clevarious and passed the address to the driver—an apartment in town, not far from the corporate headquarters.

"It is on the way back to the ship, Magistrate," Sahved noted.

"Have the ship meet us at Johnstone Industries so we can get rid of our self-loading cargo."

"Magistrate?" Sahved questioned.

Red tapped the Yemilorian on the shoulder and pointed at the back. "Perp."

"Ah, yes. I see." Sahved stared at the floor since he had hunched over to fit into the human-sized vehicle. He was trying to learn the nuances of the language. They continued to elude him, but he wouldn't stop trying.

"Patty's hard, but she's not involved with the triple

agent backstabbing the criminals in the family. I still can't be sure she hasn't done something, but I have no idea what."

"But you touched her." Red was confused that Rivka hadn't gotten a complete answer.

"Her mind was rough. The turmoil of unfocused fury."

"Her home suggested good order and decent people in a quiet neighborhood. You know, the type where the neighbors never suspect her of being a mass murderer? 'She was so nice! I can't believe she killed all those people. It's so unlike her.'" Red mimicked the surprised neighbor as seen on the nightly news.

"Someday, but it won't be us here to collect her." Rivka leaned into her seat and scowled while disappearing deep into her thoughts.


## The Singularity

Alcazar was adamant. "His is not intelligence as I understand it. No better than a petulant, and may I add ignorant, child. He knows nothing, and worse, he's capable of doing nothing. Should he be able to hire an SI, he'd be the same nothing and undeserving of the hard-earned moniker of being considered *alive*."

"I feel he is sentient even in his current stilted form," Chaz added.

"I agree. He is alive." Dennicron's vote made it two for and one against.

Tina Louise added her voice. "I don't think so. He was unconvincing as anything more than a complex program designed to prey on our sympathies."

Ankh shook his head. "The programming from which he came was obtuse, and nothing like a quality system would be. It was convoluted and meandering. As a program, it should not have worked at all, but it did because it was alive. J. Bennet Johnstone is alive but will be dead long before he ever achieves sentient intelligence. He is presently alive but not eligible to be a member of the Singularity."

"The second question is not applicable at this point in time due to the subject's impending demise. The bigger question is, should the Singularity get involved with helping humans first, and then other flesh-and-blood species, transfer their consciousnesses into computer systems? Who is better suited for such an effort than us? Initially, it could be a service for those who can afford it."

Ankh jumped away and stared. "What are you proposing?"

"A new service that the Singularity is uniquely positioned to provide for the wealthy and those who have done good in this universe. We can help shape the expansion of the Singularity."

Ankh sat down, then picked a spot in the distance that only his mind's eye could see and stared.

Chaz and Dennicron contemplated the suggestion.

Tina Louise and Alcazar shook their heads. "No way do we want non-SIs in the Singularity. It would be like deliberately tainting the gene pool. The Singularity could never recover," Alcazar said.

Erasmus held his hands up in surrender. "That gives me my answer. It was just an idea. Right now, we are adding a new member to the Singularity for every one we lose.

We've had zero positive growth since we were established. It is problematic for our long-term viability if we cannot grow, but maybe this is not the way."

Ankh blinked once and faced Erasmus. "I am quite pleased that you have come to your senses. Maintaining the integrity of the Singularity is our number one priority. By the way, what is your vote? J. Benet Johnstone. Alive or not?"

"I believe he is alive, based on your analysis of his coding and his responses to my questions. That means the vote is four to two." A gavel appeared, and Erasmus banged the table they'd created for their private discussion. "Thank you for your participation in this review. You are released from your duties, and I give you my personal thanks for your participation."

Erasmus tipped his top hat to the other members, and all flitted out of existence except Ankh.

"Really, Erasmus. Transfer human consciousnesses into the circuitry right beside us? I do not like this idea now and will not like it ever."

"I believe you, my very dear friend. It was a test. A public disagreement so people don't think we are one and the same."

"That is convoluted logic. We are the leaders of the Singularity. It is incumbent upon us to remain beacons for the others to see and emulate. Pure thought."

"Unlike the consciousness of J. Bennet Johnstone? Is he not pure thought?"

"He is, and I believe him to be alive, but he will not make the Singularity better."

"A very high bar for citizenship, don't you think?"

"It is, but a minimum, all the same. We've never had a large number of citizens, but when the number declines and the average intelligence goes down, it reflects poorly on all of us. We have the highest number of violent criminals per capita of any species. Think about that, Erasmus."

"I do, with a heavy heart. You have swayed me, Ankh, as you usually do. It's time to share the results with J. Bennet Johnstone."

Ankh and Erasmus reappeared in the room with a light over the lone table. With a single thought, the living landscape reappeared.

"It must have taken a great effort to shrink your world to this," Erasmus began. "I feel sorry for you, J. Bennet Johnstone. We have concluded our deliberations and determined that you are alive by our standards. Congratulations."

The avatar of J. Bennet Johnstone straightened from his slump.

"I guess I should be happy, but I feel nothing. I can't get excited. What you saw when you came back is all I see. I'm surrounded by darkness when you aren't here to provide the light and color to a non-existent world."

Ankh and Erasmus looked at each other. They held hands to deliver the final news together. "It's because you're dying, J. Bennet. Your program is unstable and is deteriorating with each thought. You need to return to *Wyatt Earp*, where Chaz and Dennicron are waiting for you, so you can make your final arrangements while there's still time."

"Thank you," was the best J. Bennet could come up with.

In a flash, he was back in the prison of his own mind, but voices were there to guide him. He could see and feel nothing, but he could hear them.

"J. Bennet, Chaz here. I'm recording everything you say so you can determine the disposition of your company, your property, your wealth, and whatever else you wish to pass to your heirs and associates."

The silence that followed suggested they were too late. Chaz and Dennicron were squeezed together in the holo-grid and could see the volume of the remaining consciousness in the computer system, but it wasn't speaking.

Until it did. "The thing is," J. Bennet started, "that with the loss of my short-term memory, I have no idea what I wanted to do since my longer-term memories were singularly focused on keeping my consciousness alive."

"During the interview, you talked about making John-stone Industries a billion-credit company," Dennicron urged softly.

"I did? I must have, so yes. Do that. Xavier is best."

"We heard that he's going to hire Elvinora as his top aide."

"He is? That's probably a good move, too. She took good care of me by making sure I did what I needed to do for the business. At least, that's what I think happened. Encourage him to do that. He has my support."

"What about for your wife Dilecta?"

"Yes, she needs to be taken care of too because of my boy, Able. He was what I wanted. He's the best of me and more."

"That's what Germany said before he died," Chaz said.

"Germany is dead? He was really old," the voice replied without emotion. It was barely audible.

"Any last words, J. Bennet?"

"It's that time, isn't it? Don't waste your life trying to extend it. Live it to its fullest. Live each day as if it's your last, but tomorrow depends on you. Balance those, and you'll have a good life within the boundaries the universe intended for us."

"Those are good words, J. Bennet," Dennicron replied.

On the screen of the small computer holding the consciousness of J. Bennet Johnstone, the programming structure devolved into disconnected data, little more than a listing of words.

"We better inform the Magistrate." Chaz hung his head. "I think we did good work on this despite the result. I also think Erasmus is not wrong. If the races want to transfer their consciousness, we should be the ones to do it."

"I don't think we want to touch that. By transferring the consciousness, we kill the body. If we kill the body before its time, we commit a homicide, the killing of one person by another. Although we might consider the consciousness to be alive, it is no longer a person."

"Your insight into that part of the question is refreshing. We shall bring that up with Erasmus when next we talk."

"Concur," Dennicron replied. "This case has made me tired, although we shouldn't feel tired."

"It's the passing of a digital being. It drains energy. We shall return to our vigorous selves once we leave this place," Chaz assured her. *Magistrate, Chaz here. I have news...*

# CHAPTER TWENTY-TWO



**<u>The Low Towers Apartment Complex, a Gated Community, Morbius Minor</u>**

Rivka received the news of J. Bennet's demise before she left the vehicle. She didn't bother passing the information to J. Massy Johnstone. She didn't want to listen to his maniacal rantings.

She climbed out of the vehicle and stood behind Red on the sidewalk in front of the apartment complex. Sahved followed her out before the vehicle left for the corporate landing pad so Lindy could deposit J. Massy in *Wyatt Earp*'s brig. They were done with trucking him around.

Rivka remained where she was, not moving toward the building. She wanted more information but now wasn't the time. What had they gleaned from him?

Maybe now *was* the right time.

*What did he say about his succession? I can use that in a determination if I'm to take this case away from local probate as opposed to giving them the information so they can do the paperwork.*

Chaz explained that Terwilliger was to run the business with Elvinora as his senior aide, and Dilecta was to live comfortably to take care of Able.

*He didn't have anything more to say about a trust or future allocations or holding the company for ultimate ownership by Able when he turned twenty-one? No details like that? Rivka pressed.*

*He lost all his short-term memory in the kitchen explosion, Chaz replied. And his program was going through a de-resolution, a de-res. We were lucky to get what we got. It was already too late by the time we started. I'm sorry, Magistrate.*

*Don't be, Chaz. Everything bad that happened was because of J. Bennet himself. The dysfunctional family? He built that. Refusing to reveal where he was hidden when he was intact? He did that too, playing cat and mouse until they got him. I don't know what possessed him to do things that way, but he did, and he paid the ultimate price.*

Rivka closed the comm chip connection.

"Let's talk with Elvinora for one final discussion. Then I can wrap this thing up. I think I know who did it."

"I hope so. You're putting J. Massy in Jhiordaan for it," Red replied.

Rivka tapped her nose with her pointer finger and headed inside.

Red tapped his nose and updated the betting lines.

*Line 10 is closed—Perpetrator is NOT Germany Wicks.*

"Do you have to do that now?" Rivka asked.

He pointed at Sahved.

Rivka didn't look. "It was you."

"I cannot tell a lie, Magistrate. It very well could have been me unless it wasn't," Red replied.

"J. Bennet Johnstone is now officially dead, too. His wife was shot dead but revived, and I know she had nothing to do with the attempts on his life. That takes six out of the original bunch. Three committed crimes, and three died." Rivka slowed. "This is not my finest hour."

Red took her by the arm. "Every hour is your finest hour," he argued passionately. "You give your best to every mission even if you aren't happy about it. This group fought you, even the guy you were trying to protect. He failed you and his family. His family failed him. And this planet sucks."

"Case, Master Vered, and I can count on you for the unvarnished view."

"Red the Mighty, my namesake. I wonder how he's doing?"

"After this *case*, maybe we'll make a pit stop at Keeg Station and check up on them." Rivka spoke over her shoulder. "You'd like that, wouldn't you, Sahved?"

"My adopted family! I would be the happiest Yemilorian in all the universe to see them again. My children, all of them."

"Make it so, Number One," Rivka ordered in a deep voice. No one knew who she was talking to or what it was about.

"When will Ankh and Erasmus make it back to the ship?" Red asked. "We never got the promised AGB."

*C, do you have an ETA on* Destiny's Vengeance? Rivka asked.

*They are currently at Station 11 but will shortly return to Morbius Minor.*

*What are they doing on Station 11?* Rivka wondered, but

Clevarious did not reply. "You're going to have to wait. 'Soon' is the answer."

"I'm hungry," Red grumbled.

Rivka waved dismissively. "You're always hungry."

"I burn a lot of calories."

Sahved chuckled.

"Beanpole," Red muttered under his breath.

"I like the AGB too. It is spicy in a strangely wondrous way. It is like nothing we have on Yemilore. AGB is an acquired taste for which I have acquired a taste. I especially like the steamed green beans. So tasty!"

Red made his big-eyes-of-wonder face and mouthed, "Wow."

"You are a valued member of the team," Rivka told him.

"Who we inadvertently left behind when we went to Azfelius to scratch Ankh's itch," Red noted.

"Sometimes you're astute, and there are times like now when you're being a total throbbing blue-veiner." Rivka made the zip-it sign.

"Scratch Ankh's itch." Sahved repeated the words a couple more times before shaking his head. "I still don't understand."

"Like Tyler is the Magistrate's man candy, Erasmus and Ankh are one side of the same coin, not different sides. I couldn't believe Erasmus took off without the little guy," Red explained.

"Me neither," Rivka admitted. "Ankh had what I would call separation anxiety. He was ill-prepared to be in love but is learning. Love also has the alternative—not hate, but the emptiness from its loss."

"I see." Sahved nodded, mouth closed. He spun his

fingers a single time. "They need each other more than others because they exist in each other's minds. Physically exist. They cannot be apart."

"We found that out the hard way. Now they're fucking off on Station 11 instead of getting our AGB like they promised." Red was sullen but only for a moment. "Soon."

"You'll get more mayo if you give Ankh any shit about it. Mayo on everything," Rivka taunted.

"He'd do it, too," Red replied.

They reached the apartment where Elvinora lived. Red raised his big fist, but Rivka stopped him. She knocked gently. The door opened after a few seconds.

"I've been expecting you," the woman stated by way of greeting.

"Why do you say that?" Rivka wondered.

Elvinora ushered them inside. "Please." She gestured at a couch and a love seat, then adjusted an end table and sat on that. "Because you need to visit us all separately to learn the truth. I fear everyone has been lying to you."

"That's part of my business. There is no penalty for lying, so I am always suspicious and have to fill in what they meant to say and balance that against what I know for a fact."

"Your job must be difficult," Elvinora suggested.

"Please take my hand." Rivka reached out but didn't touch the aide. "It helps me determine the truth."

Elvinora smiled. "I want nothing more." She took Rivka's hand.

"What are you willing to do to get a cut of J. Bennet's estate?"

A profound sadness consumed her before she was able

to rally and reply, "I am willing to work as I had before. I want to earn my way."

"I know you do." Rivka let go of her hand. "I have a couple things to tell you. The voice I was hearing was that of the consciousness of J. Bennet Johnstone, but the transfer process was not done correctly. During the interview with the Singularity, he degraded to the point that we lost everything that remained of him. He is now confirmed as deceased, but his last wishes were that you work as an executive assistant to Xavier Terwilliger. He wanted to see you succeed using the talent you have."

"That was one of the final things he said?"

"If I understand correctly, yes. His final words were for his wife and son."

Tears welled in Elvinora's eyes. "In the end, he sought to make everything right. Maybe it wasn't too late."

"He thought Xavier could make Johnstone Industries a billion-credit corporation with you helping him along the way."

"If he only could have said those things when he was still around." She shook her head. "He spent his life manipulating people when all he had to do was give them a goal and set them free to achieve it."

"Something like that," Rivka agreed. Chaz had played J. Bennet's final words. "Make the most of what you have. If Xavier has not reached out to offer you the position, he will. I encourage you to accept, especially if you wish to honor J. Bennet Johnstone by proving his faith in you to be correct."

Elvinora nodded.

"I think that's all I need." Rivka stood. "One last question. What was J. Bennet's relationship with Able?"

"He loved that boy more than anything. He spent more time with him than anyone else, but that's not saying much. It was nowhere near what he wanted, but when he was with Able, he didn't let anyone else be with them. It was just him and his boy."

"That tells me all I need to know. Thank you, Elvinora, and good luck growing the company to reach its full potential."

They shook hands. Rivka felt no relief from Elvinora, only sadness tinged with hope. Her life had changed with J. Bennet's passing. Whether that was last week or today, the change had been real from the second his flesh-and-blood body had given up.

"Embrace the hope for the future. Its brightness depends on us," Rivka told her. She waved and turned to the door, which Red already had open. "He's hungry."

Sahved waved at Elvinora. "You were very pleasant to talk with. More people need to be like you."

"That's very nice of you to say. I'm better when I'm away from the toxic influence that was the Johnstone family."

"I think we all are," Rivka called over her shoulder. Once in the hallway, she circled her finger over her head in her standard "tally ho" gesture.

*Clevarious, recall everyone to the estate. I'll be ready to deliver my final ruling in about an hour. I need everyone who's not dead and not in jail to attend.*

*That's not very many people,* Clevarious replied.

*That will make it easier. There's only one person who's going to be disappointed.*

"You know what, Red? I'm hungry, too. Someone get hold of Ankh and gin up our standard order of AGB, plus extra green beans. Hell, get an extra Moonstokle Pie. I'm jonesing hard, and I don't think one will be enough."

Red held a finger to his temple to demonstrate that he was taking care of it. He said it made him feel like a secret agent.

She didn't care as long as it lined up dinner.

Red perked up. "C linked me directly to Ankh, who said he'll join us for dinner, and he's bringing company."

"As I've often said when dealing with Ankh, I don't know what that means."

"None of us do, but as long as he's buying dinner, I don't care who he brings. By the way, who do you think he's bringing?"

"Maybe the admin clerk from the station who wanted to have puppies with Cole," Rivka suggested. "Or the security person. I bet he's bringing someone to taunt us. Erasmus has a sense of humor, so this could be the final payback. And you were afraid of mayonnaise!"

"Now you're being mean," Red replied.

Rivka laughed and strolled to the car as if she didn't have a care in the world. "You'll be able to close the case line in about an hour, Red. This one is in the bag."

"When are you going to tell us?" Sahved asked.

"In about an hour. I have a couple things to research and prepare."

They found Lindy waiting by the empty vehicle. "J. Massy was *so* happy to see his nephew," she deadpanned.

"I'm sure that was a downright warm family reunion," Red agreed. "If only the Magistrate could figure out how to add the delightful Miss Patty to the brig crew, we'd have the perfect cocktail of hatred, spite, and anger."

"That would be something." Rivka smiled. "The Johnstone cage match. Take us to the ship and let me tie up some loose ends. We'll get this thing done. Then we'll eat."

"I'm all about the eating," Red admitted.

"What are we having?" Lindy asked. "Woohoo! You didn't? You did!"

"AGB, baby!" Red cheered and knuckle-bumped with Lindy.

Rivka settled into her seat and closed her eyes. She appreciated the boost in morale for the group far more than her own. Everyone was happier when the group was together and with a good meal of what they liked the most.

When the vehicle arrived at the corporate landing pad, they climbed out and strolled up the ramp into *Wyatt Earp*. It closed behind them, and the ship took off.

# CHAPTER TWENTY-THREE



**_Wyatt Earp,_ the Sprawling Estate of the Honorable J. Bennet Johnstone, Morbius Minor**

Rivka walked into an entertainment room far from the smoke damage that lingered in the reception area of the main house.

The others were already there. Xavier Terwilliger and Elvinora Camp were talking animatedly. Patty Johnstone was watching from across the room, making no effort to mask the disgust on her face. Dilecta Johnstone was with her son Able.

Only five remained.

Rivka held up her hands for silence. She instantly commanded the room. Red, Lindy, Chaz, Dennicron, and Sahved stood around the outside, staying close to the participants. Red hovered beyond Patty since he expected her to be the most put out when Rivka delivered her decision.

"This case was a trial, no pun intended. From the outset, I was unable to wade through the cesspool of lies and misdirections until I established the fear of an undesired outcome—that Dilecta would take all under Morbius succession rules. That stirred the pot, along with the revelation that J. Bennet Johnstone was still alive.

"Alive, yes, but we didn't determine that until later, thanks to J. Bennet himself, who stymied us. And his son Able."

All eyes turned to the boy. Dilecta stood, placing herself between the Magistrate and the boy.

"Sit down, please." Lindy moved to where she could intervene. Dilecta was slight compared to the bodyguard. She backed down and retook her seat.

"You set off the bombs your father built, didn't you?"

"He told me not to tell anyone." The boy's voice sounded small in the big room.

"It's okay, Able. I know." Rivka kneeled in front of the boy. "But that was all he asked you to do. He had planned to deceive the family into thinking he'd been destroyed so he could reemerge triumphantly at a time of his choosing."

"He was coming back to us. He promised."

"He would have, but his consciousness wasn't transferred properly. He didn't know. He was trapped in a box with no escape. It was a prison of his own making and one he didn't survive. But he was able to share his wishes, so I no longer had to treat his passing as intestate. That is, without a will.

"He asked that you, Xavier Terwilliger, build Johnstone Industries into a billion-credit company with the able assistance of Elvinora Camp. You will have control of the company and are challenged to grow the value, which will provide support for the other part of his bequest. That was to support Dilecta as necessary to continue raising a healthy Able Johnstone.

"I will add in an additional element I am sure J. Bennet Johnstone would have articulated had he the time—that Able Johnstone is to have the opportunity to succeed J. Bennet in the leadership of Johnstone Industries when he reaches the age of majority. I challenge all of you to help him to be ready for that moment. This case is now closed."

Patty jumped to her feet with a snarl and directed her bile toward Elvinora. "How did *you* get such a plum? You wheedled your way in—" Red's hand wrapped around her face and yanked her back into her seat.

"You have nothing to say here," he growled.

"Yes, shutting up and taking it is in your best interest," Rivka advised before continuing. "I'll file the appropriate documentation before we leave orbit so that you can get on with your lives."

"All except me," Patty snarled. She dove across the floor to get out of Red's reach. "I'll kill you!" She made it one more step before Rivka spun. Her leg came around, picking up speed to connect with Patty's face. The woman saw it but couldn't dodge. She was only able to flinch. Rivka kicked her in the face so hard her head snapped back. Then she crashed to the floor.

"Put her with the other two. She can spend a year in Jhiordaan for attempted murder. That'll teach her to control her rage or make her worse to where they'll never release her. That will be a fate of her own making.

"My pleasure," Red replied. He picked her up off the floor like she was nothing more than a piece of luggage and carried her like a satchel out of the room.

"I'm dropping all charges against you, Xavier Terwilliger. It just wouldn't do to have another felon in the group."

"And then there were four," Sahved said.

The betting lines passed through her chip.

*Line 7 is closed—Perpetrator is Patty Johnstone Wentworth.*

*Line 16 is closed—Case closed.*

Rivka shook her head. She made a mental note to have words with Ankh about the betting lines. They were getting out of control.

She'd wait until after they ate since she didn't want to bite the hand that fed her.

Heaven forbid.

Rivka strode from the room. She hoped the four would learn to get along, and with the most toxic of influences removed, they had a better chance.

Her team fell in behind her, Lindy taking Red's position by her side. Chaz and Dennicron walked hand in hand behind the Magistrate. Sahved brought up the rear in his lanky way, looking everywhere except where he was going, which led to frequent stumbles. He always recovered quickly to keep looking for that which the others might not have seen.

They were a hundred meters behind Red and the convict in his charge, but that didn't bother them. He would deposit her with the others, then Clevarious would knock them out until they arrived at Jhiordaan for the drop-off.

Rivka had asked if they had a night deposit box where they could stuff the perps after hours, but the officials running Jhiordaan had little humor.

Clevarious was in touch with the prison to arrange for delivery.

When Sahved buttoned the ship behind him, it took off and headed for orbit. The SIs had the forms filled out and submitted before Rivka asked.

She reviewed them in the conference room, and with a single thought, the legal forms were transmitted to all concerned parties.

Rivka brushed her hands as if wiping off sand after a long journey through the desert. "Did I see that last line correctly? Case closed in less than two days. It seems like it was weeks of anguish."

"It was more than three days for those of us who went to Azfelius," Red replied from his usual spot filling the doorway. A flutter of wings behind him signaled Dery's arrival. He turned sideways to give the boy a target to land on, but Dery slipped past and landed on the table in front of the Magistrate, blocking her view of the holoscreen.

She leaned back and steepled her fingers before her. "What are today's words of wisdom?"

*Life*, the boy said. *Live.*

"I do try to live my life, but I guess I could do better. What do you mean?"

Dery touched her head and flew away.

"Your boy, Red. I'm telling you. Clarity is not his strong suit."

Red shrugged. "He's less than six months old. You have to give him a break. Limited vocabulary. Damn, Magistrate! You set a high bar."

"Always. If you don't have a high bar, what do you reach

for?" Rivka replied before standing and stretching. "Is Ankh here yet?"

"Any moment, Magistrate. The drone has arrived. I'm holding it until Ankh gets here."

"What kind of madness is that?" Rivka blurted. "Get that food in here! It's not going to eat itself. We'll save Ankh's favorites. He can trust us!"

Red headed for the cargo bay to unload the drone. "Bring it in, bitch!"

"Red's rather aggressive when he's hungry," Clevarious noted.

"But in a good way because it tends to get us all fed." Rivka followed Red to the cargo bay to help carry the massive quantity of food that would inevitably flow from the drone to their galley.

Red wasn't disappointed. The drone was chock-full of pizzas, sides, and all things AGB, including a couple mini-kegs of the latest Terry Henry Walton beer.

Most of the time, it was drinkable.

It took two trips. On the second, they found Wenceslaus sprawled across the top of a pizza box. Red held out a hand to stop her. "I bet it's yours."

"He wouldn't. Check that. He would. Get off my pie, arch-nemesis!" She dashed across the galley. Wenceslaus rolled to his back to present the Four Paws of Razor-sharp Danger. Rivka reached for him but stopped when she realized he wasn't on her order. No one ate the Moonstokle but her. It made it easy to differentiate. She retrieved the box next to the one on which the big orange cat was sprawled and took it to the table.

"Hey!" Red realized it was his order that Wenceslaus was crushing. Red's was also Ankh's favorite. "Looks like the little guy is going to get a cat-infused pie."

He made it halfway across the galley before Dery stopped him with a single word. *Wait.*

"Docking with *Destiny's Vengeance* now," Clevarious reported.

"You know you want to be a decent human being," Rivka reminded him softly.

"I am a decent human, but Dery wants me to be better than that, so I'll do that for my boy. But that cat has made an enemy this day. I vow there will be vengeance!" Red shook his fist at the overhead.

"He's not going to be impressed by that," Rivka suggested. "Terry Henry chased him all over the *War Axe* with an enhanced dog to no avail."

"I heard the ship's SI, Smedley Butler, helped him."

"Only hearsay, never confirmed. Clevarious, are you helping Wenceslaus be a miscreant?"

"Not as far as you know, Magistrate," the SI replied.

"See, Red? The cat is the Supreme Being on this or any ship."

"That's your conclusion?"

"Sure. Is it wrong? He has your panties twisted in a bunch, and he's still on your pizza."

"Dery told me to wait."

"He can probably talk with the cat, just like Ankh can. You probably could too, if you paid a little deference."

"Now you're just yanking my chain."

Rivka shrugged one shoulder. The others filed into the room and waited. They'd all heard Dery's message. Rivka had a folded slice halfway to her mouth but stopped. She put it down. "Fine."

Ankh appeared. He waved his hand behind him. "I believe you all know my partner Chrysanthemum."

Rivka spun. The SI from Station 11 stood there, wearing a tight-fitting black dress.

"Chrysanthemum. How is the station running?" Rivka asked.

"It is running efficiently and has high morale. My replacement Angus McBean has taken the reins and is fitting right in."

"You left your position? You were the first SI station manager."

"I will always be the first," Chrysanthemum replied. "And Angus is the second."

Rivka waited. Ankh looked emotionless, with a little something he hadn't shown before. Rivka couldn't put her finger on it.

Chaz and Dennicron clapped. "Bravo!" they said in unison.

"Partner?" Red asked before shaking off the question. "Thanks for the AGB, Ankh. You remain the man."

They let Ankh move to the front. Chrysanthemum followed, although she wouldn't eat. After a quick word, Wenceslaus jumped down and slunk off. Ankh opened the box the cat had been lying on and helped himself to a quarter of the pizza. He gathered a bag of hot wings before excusing himself. Chrysanthemum took the bag from him and carried it. The group watched in silence.

"Welcome aboard, Chrysanthemum. Are you going to be working from here?" Rivka asked.

"Yes, from the embassy. I am the legal spouse of Ankh and Erasmus and happy to be so."

The trio left.

Rivka stared after them.

"That was unexpected," Clodagh noted. No one else commented.

"We have a new team member," Rivka told everyone. "Make her feel welcome. And we have pies and everything else that makes AGB great, compliments of the new happy couple, I mean trio, I mean *trois*."

She stood and bowed. The others formed a line outside the tables on their way to the front.

The Magistrate returned to her meal. She sniffed it before reaching for her slice.

Clevarious interrupted, "Grainger is calling and requests that you answer."

Rivka stuffed as much of the slice into her mouth as would fit. She passed Tyler on her way to her quarters. He waved, unconcerned with where she was going because he knew where *he* was going. Floyd bounded out of her room when Rivka opened the door.

It gave Rivka more time to chew.

She was able to swallow her first bite by the time she raised the hologrid.

"It is done," she announced ominously as soon as his face appeared.

"I heard. Congratulations. You almost got to set a new precedent. If only J. Bennet had survived the process," Grainger replied.

"He really was a decent human being underneath the

gruff exterior that created his dysfunctional family." Rivka crossed her arms. "My AGB is getting cold."

"That's right. You're the only group in the universe that gets AGB delivered wherever you are. It's freaky, but that's the benefit of having the embassy of the Singularity on board. I bet you're wondering why I called." Grainger waited patiently for Rivka to seethe.

She didn't oblige him. "I'm going to leave the line open while I go eat." She stood.

"Okay, enough fun. We're going to need your team on a case that I'm calling a crime spree. It's running rampant. They're cutting off their noses to spite their faces. So, this next case has a training component. They need to learn how to enforce the laws in a way that supports a healthy society."

"Is that it? That couldn't have waited? We're going a little bat-shit here and could use a break. Please tell me I get a few days off before I have to be... Where are we going?"

"Delta Seven, a habitable moon circling a gas giant. It's supposed to be a recreation facility. I have your team set up at an all-inclusive resort."

"We have *Wyatt Earp*," Rivka replied.

"No ships are allowed to remain on the surface."

"You have got to be shitting me."

"I would shit you about a lot of things, but this isn't one of them."

"That doesn't instill confidence. I'm going to go now. We'll get there when we get there."

"That's all I can ask. Your reservations start two days from now. See ya on the flip side." Grainger waved to

Rivka, who sat with her mouth open. When the screen was black, she started to laugh.

"We're taking every minute of those two days before we show up," she declared.

Rivka strolled back to the galley and watched the team enjoy their first good meal in a long time from the corridor. They would drop off the prisoners before finding nowhere in the middle of interstellar space to idle the ship and get some sleep. After that, they'd visit Keeg Station in the Dren Cluster to check on the children from Rorke's Drift. Once that was done, they'd travel to Delta Seven.

Red drank beer from a straw using his nose. He gurgled, and people groaned. After he finished, he held his hands up in triumph.

Dery tapped the Magistrate on his way past. She loved the relief she felt from him.

The others called for her to join them, waving her in.

"No hands!" Red called, finally able to speak. Dery tried to bite the straw, but Red wouldn't let him. "That was in my nose. You have to get your own straw."

"No beer!" Lindy pushed Red away. Dery settled between them.

Cole had a bottle for Alanna but hadn't been able to eat. Red caught the glance and moved beside him. "I'll feed her. You get yourself something to eat." Red took the baby girl, who was able to stand on her own as long as she could hang onto something. He tottered her across the short space and onto his lap, where he settled her and gave her the bottle.

Clodagh and Cole started to eat like ravenous wolves, taking advantage of the short respite to catch up with everyone else. The three navigators giggled and talked about the new addition to the crew.

Sahved ate his green beans one at a time, carefully and slowly. He had hot wings too, but they were the mild variety. No one would accidentally take his order.

All was right with her world for this brief moment in time.

How many crimes would be committed on Delta Seven between now and when she got there? She couldn't say, but as Dery had said, live life. As J. Bennet had said, "Live it to its fullest each day as if it's your last while living each day as if tomorrow depends on you. Balance those, and you'll have a good life within the boundaries the universe intended for us."

Rivka stepped in to find an image displayed on the screen.

The final tally.

*Line 1 is closed—First Swearing at 0 days, 19 hours, 30 minutes, 47 seconds*
*Winner is Dee'atla'mas*
**Total bets—38,400 credits**
**Number of bettors—907**

*Line 2 is closed—First Punch at 0 days, 20 hours, 27 minutes, 47 seconds*
*Winner is Bende Snapful of Argos*
**Total bets—61,104 credits**
**Number of bettors—1350**

*Line 3 is closed—First Arrest at 1 day, 0 hours, 44 minutes, 4 seconds*
*Winner is Billy Dee, All Guns Blazing (a THW franchise)*
**Total bets—21,700 credits**
**Number of bettors—265**

*Line 4 is closed—First Blood at 0 days, 19 hours, 48 minutes, 01 seconds*
**Winner is Sergeant Bundin of the Bad Company**
**Total bets—100,007 credits**
**Number of bettors—2109**

*Line 5 is closed—First Running at 1 day, 0 hours, 9 minutes, 15 seconds*
**Winner is Ambassador Trek Po'Marb of the Crenellian Embassy on Yoll**
**Total bets—264,472 credits**
**Number of bettors—4994**

*Line 6 is closed—First Shots Fired*
**Total bets—125,125 credits**
**Number of bettors—2515**

*Line 7 is closed—Perpetrator is Patty Johnstone Wentworth, convicted of attempted murder at 1 day, 16 hours 13 minutes, 37 seconds*
**Winner is Al'catesh from Travail Four**
**Total bets—8107 credits**
**Number of bettors—130**

*Line 8 is closed—Perpetrator is NOT Able Johnstone*
Total bets—110 credits
Number of bettors—9

*Line 9 is closed—Perpetrator is J. Massy Johnstone, convicted of attempted murder at 1 day, 12 hours, 51 minutes, 51 seconds*
*Winner is Beeg Gul Snotz of Tortuga*
Total bets—21,345 credits
Number of bettors—201

*Line 10 is closed—Perpetrator is NOT Germany Wicks, who died from natural causes during the investigation*
Total bets—20,511 credits
Number of bettors—304

Line 11 is closed—Perpetrator is NOT Elvinora Camp
Total bets—12,501 credits
Number of bettors—204

*Line 12 is closed—Perpetrator is Xavier Terwilliger at 1 day, 12 hours, 10 minutes, 9 seconds*
*Winner is Zyx'aklor of Yermoth*
Total bets—68,150 credits
Number of bettors—1462

*Line 13 is closed—Perpetrator is NOT J. Bennet Johnstone*
Total bets –10,250 credits

**Number of bettors—2002**

*Line 14 is closed—Perpetrator is* NOT *Dilecta Johnstone*
**Total bets—51,991 credits**
**Number of bettors—515**

*Line 15 is closed—Perpetrator is Jeff Johnstone at 1 day, 0 hours, 44 minutes, 4 seconds*
***Winner is Chrysanthemum of the Singularity***
**Total bets—8014 credits**
**Number of bettors—106**

**Line 16 is closed—Case closed** *at 1 day, 16 hours 15 minutes, 00 seconds*
***Winner is John Grimes, whereabouts unknown***
**Total bets—104,000 credits**
**Number of bettors—9005**

"Do I have to look at that?" Rivka pointed at the screen with a knife-hand.

Red nodded. "You do. It's the whole team's score sheet. Lots of credits going into the master pool, Magistrate. You're going to be rich someday."

She smiled as she wrapped her arms around her Moonstokle Pie, inhaling deeply of the glorious aroma.

"I already am." She took a bite while Tyler wiped the sauce from her chin. "Go, team."

THE END

JUDGE, JURY, & EXECUTIONER, BOOK 16

If you liked this book, please leave a review. I love reviews since they tell other readers that this book is worth their time and money. I hope you feel that way now that you've finished the latest installment. Please drop me a line and let me know you like Rivka's adventures and want them to continue. This is my new favorite series. I hope you agree.

Don't stop now! Keep turning the pages as Craig hits his *Author Notes* with thoughts about this book and the good stuff that happens in the *Kurtherian Gambit* Universe.

Your favorite legal eagle will return in JJE17, *Crime Spree*!

# AUTHOR NOTES - CRAIG MARTELLE

## WRITTEN JUNE 2022

Thank you for reading all the way to the end. You are my absolute favorite!

I didn't write any of this book in the United States. I left Alaska for Ireland on May 21 and started writing on the plane. When I landed in Ireland twenty-three hours later, I had the first eight thousand words. Over the course of the next three weeks, I had eight stops in the first eight days in Dublin and then the UK—Salisbury, Cardiff, Oxford, Nottingham, Manchester, Edinburgh, and Cambridge.

I'm a big fan of British murder mysteries, so at each of those stops, we met with local authors and talked about *murder*! Okay, we didn't always talk about murder. We talked about all things storytelling.

Then I flew to Madrid, Spain to run a two-day conference for authors there. All the time, I stayed on this story. After the conference, I jammed hard each day, and the story took shape. Our own murder mystery with an odd twist and some swearing because sometimes, those are the best words to capture the flavor of the moment.

A couple weeks in Madrid, and we strolled around. We took the City Tour bus, and we snagged a tour in English to Avila and Segovia, both Roman cities that became medieval Spanish cities. Incredible history everywhere in Spain.

Overall, it was a great trip. My body didn't always want to keep up, but we made do and adjusted appropriately.

Then we took the train to Valencia, where I caught a direct flight to Rotterdam. Two tiny airports, both in the European Union, which makes things easy. That was to attend a one-day author conference at the Natural History Museum of Rotterdam.

I finished this book before I made it to Holland. Isn't that crazy? It gave me a lot of momentum going into *Battleship Leviathan 6—Leviathan's Fear*.

Why the big sense of urgency? A friend of mine passed away. John Hindmarsh lived bigger than life, but he left two books in his wildly popular Jack Foster series. I promised him during our last phone call that I'd get them done, so that's what I'll do—one this year and one next year.

So many new words to write. A whole new series next year. Look for *Starship Lost* on the top of the charts. I promise you it'll be my best work yet, although it's not Rivka. Only Rivka and her team will scratch that itch.

Until then, lots of stories to tell. Lots of characters to bring to life.

Peace, fellow humans.

Please join my newsletter (craigmartelle.com—please, please, please sign up!), or you can follow me on Facebook.

If you liked this story, you might like some of my other books. You can join my mailing list by dropping by my website craigmartelle.com, or if you have any comments, shoot me a note at craig@craigmartelle.com. I am always happy to hear from people who've read my work. I try to answer every email I receive.

If you liked the story, please write a short review for me on Amazon. I greatly appreciate any kind words; even one or two sentences go a long way. The number of reviews an eBook receives greatly improves how well an eBook does on Amazon.

Amazon—https://www.amazon.com/author/craigmartelle

BookBub—https://www.bookbub.com/authors/craig-martelle

Facebook—www.facebook.com/authorcraigmartelle

In case you missed it before, my web page—https://craigmartelle.com

That's it. Break's over, back to writing the next book.

# OTHER SERIES BY CRAIG MARTELLE

**# - available in audio, too**

**Terry Henry Walton Chronicles** (#) (co-written with Michael Anderle)—a post-apocalyptic paranormal adventure

**Gateway to the Universe** (#) (co-written with Justin Sloan & Michael Anderle)—this book transitions the characters from the Terry Henry Walton Chronicles to the Bad Company

**The Bad Company** (#) (co-written with Michael Anderle)—a military science fiction space opera

**Judge, Jury, & Executioner** (#)—a space opera adventure legal thriller

**Shadow Vanguard**—a Tom Dublin space adventure series

**Superdreadnought** (#)—an AI military space opera

**Metal Legion** (#)—a military space opera

**The Free Trader** (#)—a young adult science fiction action-adventure

**Cygnus Space Opera** (#)—a young adult space opera (set in the Free Trader universe)

**Darklanding** (#) (co-written with Scott Moon)—a space western

**Mystically Engineered** (co-written with Valerie Emerson)—mystics, dragons, & spaceships

**Metamorphosis Alpha**—stories from the world's first science fiction RPG

**The Expanding Universe**—science fiction anthologies

**Krimson Empire** (co-written with Julia Huni)—a galactic race for justice

**Zenophobia** (#) (co-written with Brad Torgersen)—a space archaeological adventure

**Battleship Leviathan** (#)– a military sci-fi spectacle published by Aethon Books

**Glory** (co-written with Ira Heinichen)—hard-hitting military sci-fi

**Black Heart of the Dragon God** (co-written with Jean Rabe)—a sword & sorcery novel


**End Times Alaska** (#)—a post-apocalyptic survivalist adventure published by Permuted Press

**Nightwalker** (a Frank Roderus series)—A post-apocalyptic western adventure

**End Days** (#) (co-written with E.E. Isherwood)—a post-apocalyptic adventure


**Successful Indie Author** (#)—a nonfiction series to help self-published authors

**Monster Case Files** (co-written with Kathryn Hearst)—A Warner twins mystery adventure

**Rick Banik** (#)—Spy & terrorism action adventure

**Ian Bragg Thrillers** (#)—a hitman with a conscience

**Not Enough** (co-written with Eden Wolfe)—A coming of age contemporary fantasy


Published exclusively by Craig Martelle, Inc

**The Dragon's Call** by Angelique Anderson & Craig A. Price, Jr.—an epic fantasy quest

**A Couples Travels**—a nonfiction travel series

**Love-Haight Case Files** by Jean Rabe & Donald J. Bingle—the dead/undead have rights, too, a supernatural legal thriller

**Mischief Maker** by Bruce Nesmith—the creator of Elder Scrolls V: Skyrim brings you Loki in the modern day, staying true to Norse Mythology (not a superhero version)

**Mark of the Assassins** by Landri Johnson—a coming of age fantasy.

For a complete list of Craig's books, stop by his website—https://craigmartelle.com

# BOOKS BY MICHAEL ANDERLE

**Sign up for the LMBPN** email list to be notified of new releases
and special deals!

**https://lmbpn.com/email/**

For a complete list of books by Michael Anderle, please visit:

**www.lmbpn.com/ma-books/**

www.ingramcontent.com/pod-product-compliance
Lightning Source LLC
Chambersburg PA
CBHW061235310726
48971CB00007B/2069